The Royal Diaries

Lady of Ch'iao Kuo

Warrior
of the South

BY LAURENCE YEP

Scholastic Inc. New York

Southern China
A.D. 531

Scroll One

Third Year of the Chung Ta T'ung Era
Second month, first to fourth days

Oh, no! Father has canceled the Spring Festival! I am disappointed because our people, the Hsien, come from all over the Great Forest to Kingfisher Hill, our capital, for the festival. There is singing, dancing, feasting, and games. It's ever such a marvelous time.

This year, winter has been quite dreary. I counted the days until I could come home from school. I even brought my school clothes along because my sisters wanted to see them.

I board at the school in the Chinese colony that has grown up near the silver mine. And I return home to Kingfisher Hill only for the holidays.

Father apologized for canceling the festival. It's the Dog Heads. While I was at school, they had begun sending large war bands into the Chinese colony. I should have realized they would raid here, too.

The Dog Heads have been feuding with us for centuries. They're a savage folk who take people's heads for the power they symbolize. Maybe it's because they believe their ancestor was a man with a dog's head.

They've always been jealous of the Hsien and of our village in particular. And the jealousy turned to outright poison when the Chinese came and started the silver mine twenty-three li away. Our location makes us the middlemen between all the peoples of the Great Forest and the Chinese. We've grown rich on the trade, and our wealth won us the kingship of the Hsien.

Long ago — before I was even born — Father won a great battle against the Dog Heads and taught them that the Hsien were the mightiest of all the peoples of the Great Forest. And we have been here longer than anyone can remember. Even my old nursemaid, Kumquat.

After that humiliating defeat, the Dog Heads only dared to steal a buffalo and take an occasional head of anyone who got careless. Until recently, when they started stealing and killing on a larger scale.

I wondered why Father had sent such a large escort to bring me back from school. I was surprised when he told me that he wants me to return to school. He needs someone in the Chinese colony to tell him what is happening.

When he told me this plan, Father was looking particularly kingly in his finest poncho. Mother had woven hunting patterns of floss silk through the cloth. And the tattoos on his arms and legs gleamed like tigers' stripes, making him look like the fierce warrior he is. It would have been impossible for any Hsien to say no to so regal a king.

Mother, though, shook her head so that her large silver earrings rocked like banners. And I could tell from the wrinkling of the flower patterns tattooed on her forehead that she was angry. She made it clear that in no way was she going to let me travel back through the forest.

Father, who's the bravest of the brave, usually gives in to her when she wears that expression. In public, she's always careful to go along with whatever Father says. However, in private, it's another thing. Though everyone calls my father the king, everyone knows it's Mother who is the true ruler of the tribe.

For once, though, he kept on arguing. He said I could wait and accompany a caravan of trade goods we were sending to the Hsien. The guard would be so large no Dog Head raider would attack.

Even so, Mother will not let me go.

I've been sent out of the room while they "discuss" things further.

My parents have been in their room all this time. I can hear them through their room's bamboo wall.

Father is telling Mother that they need a reliable pair of eyes and ears in the Chinese colony to make reports during a crisis like this. That is one of the reasons why they have sent me to the colonists in the first place. I have always been mature and Father mentioned Peacock's hen to prove it.

Five years ago, the best laying hen of our steward, Peacock, got through a hole in Auntie Goral's shed and ate some of her grain. Peacock wanted his hen back, but Auntie Goral said only if he gave her back the part that had the grain. Peacock said he'd give the grain back in a new form in a few days and she'd be welcome to it. That only made Auntie Goral call Peacock a thief. She was going to chop a hunk out of the hen and keep that.

Though Auntie Goral is as small as Peacock, she has strong arms and hands from her pottery-making. So there was no way Peacock could force her to surrender his hen.

The entire village took one side or the other. It got to the point where neighbors were threatening to punch one another.

All over a handful of grain!

So I said, Why not give some of the hen's eggs to Auntie Goral?

It just seemed like the reasonable thing to me, but everyone acted as if I had spoken the wisdom of the ages.

That shows how little common sense there is nowadays.

But ever since then, people had been coming to me to solve their minor spats.

Father is just happy that I take care of these little things for him.

Once when I complained to Mother about people bothering me all the time, she replied that all I had to do to lose my reputation was scratch my head and say I couldn't come up with anything.

I thought about it, but I couldn't do it. I guess I like challenges — and I like my reputation — so I kept on.

Evening

When I brought their meals into them, they both looked exhausted.

Father told me to stay, though. Then he asked Mother if she thought I was mature.

Mother said of course she did. That's why they could trust me to keep my wits and keep my temper at school.

She was sure it hadn't been easy for me at school; but so far I had proved them right.

Though she didn't say it, we all knew that my oldest brother, Little Tiger, would have been a disaster to send to the colony. Little Tiger is seventeen — a year older than me. As my big brother, he's always bullied me and our little sisters, Hibiscus and Begonia, and our little brothers, Drongo and Barbet. However, now that he has realized he's the crown prince, he's begun to bully everyone. So it wouldn't have been wise to let him loose among Chinese colonists.

Then Father sprang his trap. "Let's let Princess Redbird choose." He used my Chinese name on purpose to remind my mother that I had two lives. "But before she does, let's explain to her what's at stake."

I was so flattered to be treated like a grown-up — almost as if I were somebody important. So I said I would like to know.

Father told me then that a war between the Hsien alone and the Dog Heads was likely to be a stalemate. We are evenly matched in numbers with the Dog Heads. His last victory had been as much a matter of luck as planning and courage.

He had just said I was mature. I found out that I was not. Right then I would rather have been sheltered from the truth like a child: I want to believe Father is invincible and that he would win another victory and chase our enemies back into their hills.

So I asked Father what he was going to do.

To fight the Dog Heads, Father wants to get all the other peoples of the Great Forest to join us in an alliance! A show of force by an allied army would cow the Dog Heads and lead to a bloodless victory.

An alliance of all the peoples of the Great Forest! That's never been done. That almost made my head spin. Only a grand king like my father would think of that!

As much as I hated to, I pointed out the obvious flaw in the scheme. We had been feuding with the other tribes forever — not just with the Dog Heads. And even among the Hsien, there have been feuds between villages and families for countless generations. How could we forget all that overnight?

Mother said that was the problem. We had been feuding for so long that no one remembered the original cause. Who knows who was first at fault? The important thing is to stop this endless cycle of violence.

I asked her if we were to forget our honor and pride, too.

Mother said that honor and pride were just excuses for using brute force. That's what was wrong with the Hsien and all the other tribes: We thought force could solve everything. It's what the more warlike Hsien lords want to use against the Dog Heads. Brute force, however, was not the answer either with enemy tribes — or big brothers.

Father added that it wasn't just the Dog Heads that were the problem. If the tribes of the Great Forest want to remain free, they will have to join together, anyway. One day the Chinese were bound to put their empire back together again. The peoples of the Great Forest must unite before that can happen. Or we will disappear along with the Great Forest.

No, I'm not a grown-up yet. I can't think on that scale. It made me feel humble and yet proud at the same time — humble for my childishness but proud of my parents' vision.

Father says it will be my job to tell my parents what the Chinese are thinking and doing.

Don't misunderstand. I'm not brave at all; and two years ago if they had let me choose, I would gladly have stayed here. The last thing I wanted back then was to go among strangers who had stolen our lands and enslaved so many people.

But then I met Master Chen. And I had found his library.

And if Father thought I was doing the job of an adult by returning to the Chinese colony, then that's what I would do.

So I reminded Mother that I was not only her daughter,

but a princess. And she herself had often said that a princess has certain duties and must take certain risks.

If there is one thing Mother hates, it is to have her own words used against her. She scowled at me horribly. "Sometimes I think your memory is too good." But she gave in. Then she burst into tears.

Father just watched helplessly. He can lead a war band to victory and impress the other kings of the Great Forest; but he just gawked like a small boy now.

So I put my arms around my mother and told her that I would be fine.

She said I was already a young woman. That realization was partly why she was crying.

I told Mother that we should enjoy what moments we have together.

We're to have a picnic tomorrow! Just like in the old days.

Second month, second day
Morning

I will wear my robe of kingfisher blue. The colors are perfect since our capital is named Kingfisher Hill. The apron, cuffs, and collar are of a lovely brocade that's as red as a kingfisher's head, and the material is embroidered with phoenixes in gold thread. Sewn to the apron's hem are triangles that look like back feathers on a kingfisher. Also attached to the hem are long ribbons that match the apron.

The robe makes me feel like a kingfisher girl. The wide sleeves reach below my waist. When I whirl around, the sleeves rise into the air as if I'm flying and the ribbons swirl around me.

Though I'm wearing a belt of red Chinese cord, I've attached cowrie shells all along its length. I like how they dangle and click together.

My maid, Francolin, thinks I'm going to overheat and die. However, she's not happy unless she has something about which to worry.

On the other hand, Drongo and Hibiscus love it. They hold onto the ribbons and dance around me in a circle. And they like to see me twirl around with sleeves flapping like wings and the ribbons whipping about.

I should wear shoes, too, I know, but I don't find them very comfortable so I'll leave them off.

I have plenty of clothes from my Chinese hosts, the Chens, to outfit the rest of my family. Mother can wear one of my robes. And we can tuck up the robes for the girls. I have belts and scarves for Father and the boys. I think that's as much as I can expect them to put on.

But what about my hair? Should I bind it up in the traditional way into a fat topknot? When I first went to school, the Chens teased me by calling it the mortar pestle.

Chinese women wind their hair around wire frames to create elaborate shapes. For the sake of time, though, I think I'll just braid my hair. Francolin can help me loop the braids from the top of my head to the back of my neck. That will give some of the same effect.

Late afternoon

Our picnic started out as lovely as I could have wished. It began a bit late, however.

Dressing took much longer than I had expected. Hibiscus and Begonia both wanted their hair like mine. So Francolin and I helped them.

She thinks the mock-Chinese style odd, but she likes a challenge.

Mother surprised me by asking me to style her hair as well. However, she refused to give up her own large silver earrings for the Chinese ones. I offered her the largest Chinese ones I had, but they are still tiny in comparison.

Everyone in Kingfisher Hill turned out to see the royal family walk by dressed as Chinese. We set tongues wagging immediately.

I have read that the Chinese emperor is so special that it is death for a common person to see him. However, the

Hsien not only expect to see their king but they also speak their minds to him. So they began teasing my father. Though he was uncomfortable, he tried to hide it for my sake.

I had brought along some treats from the Chinese colony so I told our steward, Peacock, to pass out some of the surplus dumplings and meat pastries.

The joking changed into happy munching.

Our capital sits on a hill that's surrounded on three sides by a river. And I led everyone through the gates to my favorite spot. It's a grassy spot on top of the western bank before the palisade.

A dirt slope drops to the river below. It is full of holes that were the old burrows of the kingfishers from last season.

Though the kingfishers prefer to live scattered throughout the Great Forest, they like to nest here. There's so much food for them, from bugs to small fish. So they're willing to forget their feuds and dig their nests in the soft slopes. That's how our capital received its name.

It was a beautiful day — sunny but not too warm yet. Everyone nibbled the Chinese food warily at first. However, when they found it tasted good, they devoured everything in sight.

And then I got to see my first kingfisher since my arrival. There used to be far more when I was small. However, the Chinese prize their blue feathers for jewelry and clothing and even tents and canopies! They pay the Hsien well for kingfisher feathers.

The bird perched at the top of a tree across the river. It bobbed its red head. And when it spread its wings, the undersides flashed a dazzling white to match its chest.

Suddenly, the bird gave a laugh and sprang into the air. And I saw the bright, shiny blue of its back and wings and tail. There is no blue like a kingfisher blue — not even the sky can match it.

Laughing, the bird rose higher and higher. Above the trees. Above the palisade and houses. And still it soared, laughing as it climbed until it was a round dot.

And then it spiraled downward like a blue bolt of lightning to land back on its treetop. Suddenly, another kingfisher perched on a branch just below it.

Hibiscus wanted to know what they were doing. Father said the male was courting the female. Mother chuckled and said we should have seen Father when he was courting her.

It's early for it, though. Soon the air will be filled with kingfishers courting and then digging their nests in the soft dirt of the riverbank.

Father told us to remember the sight. By the time we have children, there won't be any more kingfishers. When he was a boy, the kingfisher burrows had covered both banks of the river and the noise in the morning was deafening. However, the Hsien have hunted so many of them for feathers that their numbers are dwindling. Now the kingfisher nests will probably only fill one side of the river. They have already disappeared from many parts of the Great Forest.

I have always taken the kingfishers for granted. I am horrified now to think they will vanish. I told Father that it is wrong to kill something so lovely just so the Chinese can make decorations.

He thought about that for a while, and then I'll never forget his smile. It made me feel all warm and safe. And he agreed. He was sure they had been put in this world just for our delight.

He is going to give orders. People will no longer catch the birds. Instead, we will only be allowed to gather what feathers fall. Though the feathers won't be as good.

Second month, third day
Morning

I am determined to enjoy my own advice to my mother. I want to savor every moment that I am home. As I sit on the veranda of the palace, battles seem so very far away.

The winter is giving way to spring, finally. The air is already starting to warm.

The sunlight is sparkling from the river, and the

mountains are so hazy I can barely see the grottoes where our ancestors once lived.

All around me the houses' thatched roofs gleam like fuzzy, pale gold feathers. They perch on stilts like a flock of long-legged birds. Our palace is the biggest one of all, of course. It has to be big enough to hold the council, and there are bedrooms for the family and the servants. My parents' room is just behind the council room and is the largest. It's filled with chests and wardrobes where we keep the clan's treasures.

And outside we keep the great bronze drum, the Voice of the Forest. It is the pride of the Hsien.

Verandas surround the houses on three sides. It's a warm, muggy day, so almost everyone is outside to do their chores or to play.

Most of the animals are grazing, so their pens underneath the houses are empty. However, I can hear a couple of the royal buffalo moving beneath me. They must have been kept at home because they are sick.

Smoke rises from the houses like lazy snakes sunning themselves. I can smell the yam cakes baking. Ooo, and the pork smells so good when it's roasting. I hope our chef, Toad, will cook some ducks tonight. No one can make a sugar-and-honey marinade like he can. And it's been a long time since I've had his fermented fish.

I can see a group coming through the gates. The smell of cinnamon rises from baskets that are slung behind their heads. They must have come from the trees in Cinnamon Pass. The cinnamon hearts are pieces of inner bark cut from youthful branches and are especially pungent. I think of some of Kumquat's sweets, and that makes my stomach rumble.

I've been trying all morning to start my school assignments. My teacher, Master Chen, has asked me to help him write the history of his homeland. But I don't know where to start. I'm not some famous scholar like him.

In fact, I'm the only one in Kingfisher Hill who can write.

By now, people have gotten used to the sight of their princess making strange marks on paper in the manner of the Chinese colonists. People here used to gather to watch me when I put out my brush pen, ink, ink well, and scraps of paper.

The closest thing my people have to writing is notches in a stick. But we just use those to record a trade of buffalo or grain, not our thoughts.

However, they just smile and shake their heads when they see me doing my school assignments now. Only Francolin objects to my writing, and that's because she's the one who has to clean up ink spills.

Of course, I shouldn't be wasting paper this way. But I think a day like today deserves remembering.

That is the marvelous thing about writing. I can pick up a book and read about a sunny afternoon from five hundred years ago in some Chinese village a thousand li from here. A village, which has disappeared, yet I can still visit it, anyway. What magic!

And so perhaps in a thousand years, someone will read these words and see a sunny afternoon in —

A little later

I was just interrupted by my brother, Little Tiger, and his fellow apes. They came by to complain about Father's decree on the kingfishers.

They blame me! They call it the Princess's law.

They say the Chinese have filled my head with all sorts of notions.

I tell them that the Chinese are so desperate for feathers that they will buy the fallen feathers instead.

Little Tiger got that frustrated look on his face the way he always does when he tries to argue with me. I usually wind up winning. However, the other apes were taunting him.

When a boy reaches adolescence, it's the custom

among our people to send him to join other boys his age in a separate house.

Though the Youth House is its official name, most everyone calls it the Ape House. The boys urge one another on to one worse prank after another. And they've filled Little Tiger's head with ideas about his station. So my brother's gone from awful to awfullest.

The other apes asked him if his sister was making him a weakling like the Chinese, too.

My brother is so predictable. He got all red in the face and then told me to go back to my Chinese books.

I told him not to underestimate the Chinese nor their books.

Then, instead of trying to use words and reason, he resorted to fists.

I have often gone hunting with Father so I can shoot a bow as well as any boy in the tribe. And because I have often had to wrestle my big brother I can handle myself.

Unfortunately, I hadn't learned how to wrestle four at once.

I admit that the casual observer might have thought I was losing to the boys. Especially since I had the biggest boy, Coconut, sitting on top of me while three others hit me. However, I could tell from their punches that they were weakening. So I was just resting while I waited for the right moment to destroy them.

Coconut got up before I could do that. He asked me why I wasn't crying out. I said I could handle my own problems. My parents had other things on their minds.

That made Little Tiger look guilty, and he took the other apes away before I got a chance to crush them.

It's nice having someone to explain these things to like this diary.

Later

I suppose I should tear up this page and start over but paper is so precious.

I outgrew the need for a nursemaid a long time ago. Kumquat's supposed to be taking care of my little brothers and sisters; but she's been fussing over my bruises and cuts while I try to write. It's no use complaining to Mother. She says Kumquat used to treat her the same way when she was a girl.

Kumquat knows more love songs than anyone I know; and I've never known anyone who thought so much about romance. And yet she's never married. She says she's had enough to do to raise the different generations of our family.

As clever as she is, though, she can't read or write. So she can't tell what I'm actually doing. No one can. Not even my parents. (That's why I was sent to Master Chen's school in the first place.)

Oh, no, Kumquat's getting out her herbal salves!

Sorry about that. Kumquat just daubed on a salve. It stung like a hundred bees, and made my brush jerk.

Later

As I said, the boys were lucky that I decided not to take my revenge on them this time. Since it's now raining outside, I guess I can't put off my school assignments. Master Chen will want to see my history pages when I return to school. I thought I would have all of my holidays to work on them; but now that I'm going back so much sooner than I had expected, I'll need something to satisfy him. So I'll do a rough draft here.

Chinese books are a set of scrolls, a separate one for each chapter. My teacher has one that unrolls to over eighty ch'ih! However, when I do my school exercises, it's on sheets of rough paper. Master Chen says that when I've polished it, I can copy it onto a proper scroll made from fine sheets of paper pasted together.

I doubt if that day will ever come.

However, I need to do something. But where to begin?

I guess I should try to sound like the histories in Master Chen's library. Maybe something like this . . .

Later that afternoon

We have lived in the Great Forest since our first ancestor left the mountains. Long ago, the thunder created an egg, and from that egg hatched a woman. She married a man from the far south who had come here to gather incense.

In the mountains across the stream, there are still the old grottoes where their children once stayed.

Ugh!

This won't do.

After two years of living with the colonists, I know most of them don't care a feather about us. All the Chinese historians are interested in is what the Chinese did. So I suppose I should write down what I know of them in our land.

Many generations ago, the Chinese invaded the land from the snowy north. They built a great city, Canton, to the northeast. Then the colonists spread out from there like a blight. The Great Forest was once far greater; but they chopped the trees down and slaughtered all the game.

When the tribes tried to resist, the Chinese soldiers crushed them. The survivors became slaves.

When the Chinese first invaded, my tribe fought them as fiercely as the rest. Even when we tried to live in peace with them, there were times when they made us so angry that we picked up our weapons and went to war against them. Their soldiers were bullies. Their tax collectors were leeches.

We had to send them so many things — from kingfisher feathers to rhinoceros horns and the sweet tree resins that the Chinese use in perfumes. Sometimes the taxes were so bad that we took up arms ourselves.

Though their soldiers beat us, they never destroyed us. There are too many of us. Master Chen says that an old census says the Hsien number a hundred thousand households. He estimates our number at over four hundred thousand people. And those are only the ones that the Chinese can reach and tax. There are more Hsien in the Great Forest that the Chinese have never visited. And we are just one people in the land. There are many other peoples besides us.

I could fill a book with the sins of the Chinese. However, one of my ancestors was practical. He said what's past is past. He's the one who first began to trade with the local Chinese colony and made Kingfisher Hill what it is today.

Now as long as we pay our taxes, the Chinese do not pester us. And at least in this area the slaving has stopped.

For fourteen generations, the Chinese empire stood

like a rock. Then the stone turned to sand and the Chinese empire crumbled away in the wind. For the last ten generations, the Chinese have been fighting one another. Master Chen says people starve within their empire because there is no one to work in the fields.

However, if you're one of the free people, it's a good time. The Chinese soldiers are too busy fighting one another to bother us. There used to be a garrison from the Liang emperor. However, he withdrew it three years ago to crush yet another rebel who was trying to claim the throne himself.

So the peoples of the Great Forest, which include the Hsien, are free to do what they want again. Unfortunately, that means some of the old feuds and rivalries have been revived. The Chinese forced the various peoples to keep peace. Not that they cared about us. War just made it hard for them to collect taxes. So with freedom has come constant warfare between the Hsien and all our neighbors, the Dog Heads as well as the other peoples of the Great Forest.

If the various tribes ever stopped fighting one another, we could wipe out the Chinese. However, I don't think that will ever happen. We hate the other tribes as much as they hate us.

So my father has taken a practical attitude. He says that the Chinese are here to stay.

Two years ago, my parents surprised almost everyone

when they accepted Master Chen's invitation to send a child to his school. I hated the idea myself. My face had just been freshly marked with lovely butterfly and flower designs so I was feeling very grown-up. I was ready for other things and not lessons from some foreigner.

However, my parents insisted that the royal family couldn't keep depending on interpreters. We needed to learn about our neighbors. And to do that I had to read their books. And the nearest books were at their school.

The Chinese empire once used our land as a kind of prison. They sent their troublemakers here to keep them out of mischief. Many of them were scholars like Master Chen's ancestor. His family had lived in the capital of the empire but were exiled to the little mining town of Kao-liang in the far south.

He started a school for his grandchildren and other children of the town. He was even taking Chinese girls as students which caused a minor scandal among the rest of the townsfolk.

That was nothing compared to having me come to his school, for I am both a girl and one of the forest folk.

It was hard at first. Even if I had not had Uncle Muntjac as an escort, my tattoos would have made me stand out.

I was proud of the designs on my face. Without them, how would my ancestors recognize me and help me when

I died? Among the Hsien, only servants like Francolin and Kumquat do not have marks.

I was aware of the smirks from the first day of school. And as I came to learn more and more of the language of the Chinese, I came to understand what they were saying. At the time, though, I only understood the contempt upon their faces.

As a princess of the Hsien, I would not give the Chinese the satisfaction of chasing me away.

If it had not been for Master Chen, I would have stopped going to school. When he learns something new, he smiles as happily as a baby. Unlike the other colonists, he loves to hear about my people.

When his own grandson said something about the tattoos on my face, Master Chen told him that some time in the distant past the ancestors of the Chinese had probably worn tattoos, too. And that the Chinese had nothing to be proud of for the way they had treated the forest people. Then he had taken out a switch and gave his grandson the best of nine.

Finally, he told all his family and students that I was a princess among my own people. And according to the Chinese legends, the Empress Nü Kua made all humans from dirt and mud. So that makes us all the same.

I love the stories about Nü Kua and the other marvelous creatures. I stayed with the lessons so I could read the marvelous tales in his library.

Master Chen knows that and he holds out the fantasy books and wonder tales like honey sweets to get me to do the rest of my work.

And so even though I must put on those stuffy Chinese robes and suffer the insults of the townsfolk, I look forward to reading tales of wonder and marvels.

I always go to the part of the bookcase where he keeps the wonder stories. Master Chen says that these tales began with simple sentences in the official histories. They were omens and strange events that foretold some change or disaster.

Then writers began to expand those sentences, describing people and places. And finally, people began writing them for their own sake.

That's the most amazing thing of all. That there was once a time when the Chinese could just make up stories and write them down.

They didn't have to be afraid of enemies attacking. They could make gardens instead of forts. They could walk out at night without any weapons and look up at stars.

Master Chen calls it "peace."

It is hard to think there really is such a thing. I find it

easier to believe that a warrior can fly through the stars in a magic chariot. However, the history books and Master Chen all say peace really existed.

Whenever I visited home, I used to tell my little brothers and sisters some of the tales I read. My little brothers, Drongo and Barbet, especially liked the stories about dragons. My little sisters, Begonia and Hibiscus, prefer stories where people travel into the fairy realms. So I sometimes have to switch back and forth.

One time, I told them about that wonderful time and place called peace.

Little Tiger heard me and just laughed. He says that peace for the Chinese is bought only by crushing people like the Hsien. Freedom is more important.

But why can't the Hsien have both?

Isn't that what Father's working for when he wants to unite the tribes of the Great Forest?

No, no, no!

This is not like the Chinese histories at all. And it insults Master Chen's people. Anyway, Chinese historians never record other people. They only write about their own kind.

I guess I'll recopy some of the kinder words about the Chinese. Then I'll tear out the page and give Master Chen that.

I hope that will be enough.

Tonight I did a Chinese dance for everyone outside the palace.

To do it properly, you need a dancing costume of white grass linen, which is a kind of stiff, strong cloth.

The key is your carriage. You're not supposed to really dance but to float as if you were a fluffy seed drifting on the breeze. At the same time, I moved my arms so that my sleeves billowed like a swan's wings slowly beating as they caught the wind.

Then I leaned my head to the side and pivoted gracefully. All around me I saw faces smiling in the firelight. Even though I did not do it as well as even Master Chen's granddaughters, my audience could not tell the difference.

However, suddenly I saw that Little Tiger was scowling. He hates anything Chinese. His frown almost threw me off, but I kept on.

Fortunately, the next step called for me to raise my sleeves and cover my face so he was hidden.

I made a point of turning my back to him as I quickened the pace. Raising and lowering my arms, I whipped the sleeves about like snowflakes in a strong wind.

However, Little Tiger began to shout rude comments. I stumbled and stopped.

Things might have ended in another fight, but Mother

jumped to her feet. From the big knot of hair at the back of her head, Mother pulled the great golden hairpin. It's as long as her forearm. The knob at the top is shaped like a butterfly and its wings taper to two sharp points.

Then she began to beat the great bronze drum hanging before the palace. The Voice of the Forest boomed like thunder. Everyone cheered. When I was small, I thought that's how a god must speak.

Little Tiger and the other boys swept in and started to stamp their feet in one of the Hsien dances.

When Mother turned over her place to someone else, she beckoned to me, saying she wanted a massage. I followed her over to a spot a little apart from everyone.

As I knelt behind her and began to rub her back and arms, Father came over and told my mother he had never heard her play better.

However, he had been using the compliment as an excuse to talk to me with Mother where the others couldn't overhear.

Then Mother explained that Little Tiger didn't mean to do these things. He was just scared the other boys would think he was too weak to be the future king.

I've never thought about that, but I guess it's true. But that only makes Little Tiger's bullying worse, and I said so.

Father sighed and said it was up to other people to

teach my brother that lesson — just as Father had learned it when he was young.

However, I didn't see why he couldn't just tell Little Tiger that.

Father explained that he could do that but it would just be words. It was a lesson that had to be learned through deeds. A prince had to do things because he felt it was right, not because he was told to do so by someone else.

I don't see why Little Tiger always gets to be the child and I always have to be the adult.

Scroll Two

Third Year of the Chung Ta T'ung Era
Second month, fifth to fourteenth days

Second month, fifth day
En Route to Kao-liang

I haven't been able to write before this. I'm doing this during the caravan's first break on the way to town. There's a stream to provide water for the ink. And fortunately the sky is clear.

Before I left Kingfisher Hill, we were already getting some bad news. The other tribes of the forest have been refusing an alliance! Father expects everyone to turn down his invitation.

The fools!

Because our territory is the closest to the Dog Heads, they think they are safe. They can't see that if we fall, it will be their turn next.

I said they were selfish idiots who couldn't see beyond their navels.

Father, though, says that we are only reaping our own harvest. For generations, the Hsien have bullied the other tribes because we are the biggest and strongest.

Just as Little Tiger bullies the other children. I wouldn't trust him, either, if he suddenly became friendly.

When I left, Father had his usual good advice. I must remember that I am a princess of the Hsien. People will judge my people by how I act . . . and so forth and so forth. I think I have the speech memorized by now.

I love walking through the Great Forest! The tall trees soar on either side of me and high overhead their branches weave together like a roof. And the sunlight falls through the leaves in a warm, green light.

I feel like a fish resting at the bottom of a pond.

A monkey calls. A parrot squawks. Leaves rustle. Something slithers in the branches above. A thousand sounds. Life is everywhere in a soft, shadowy jumble.

And yet I see nothing but the greenness. I feel as if I were in a womb. Surrounding me are all the creatures of the world waiting to be born. And I am just one of them.

Far overhead in the tree canopy, I know brightly colored flowers grow in the sun. Insects buzz. Animals play. But I can't see them, either.

The green holy light swallows up everything. Even us.

The Chinese colonists are scared of the forest. They would not last a day within the shadowy trees, but to the Hsien it's home. I think that's why some of the colonists are scared of me, too.

Up until now it's always been just old Uncle Muntjac who's escorted me. He's a veteran warrior who had taught my father the finer points of swordsmanship. However, his war and hunting stories keep getting wilder and grander every year.

On the strength of his earlier visits with me, Uncle Muntjac has been playing the guide and teacher. He's telling the caravan escort about their princess.

The other warriors think I'm soft because I called a halt. They're muttering that I've lived too much among the Chinese.

However, I only take it slower because of Uncle Muntjac. He has an old injury from a Dog Head arrowhead that makes him limp sometime.

I can't see Kingfisher Hill anymore. I always feel sad when I leave home. I miss my parents and my little brothers and sisters. I miss old Kumquat and all her love songs.

I even miss my horrid ape of a big brother.

Early afternoon

Poor Uncle Muntjac. He's already limping along badly. I could see he couldn't keep up the pace so I ordered another stop. I said I was tired because it would devastate him if I told the other warriors that I didn't think he could keep up.

Everyone's smirking. They're sure that I've grown flabby among the Chinese. Let them think what they like.

I can stand the humiliation better than Uncle Muntjac can.

He has kept me company among the Chinese without ever complaining. When I first went there, I despaired of ever learning their language and their customs. It was he who gently reminded me that this was my duty. And when I would feel homesick, he used to fetch back the wild litchi nuts I love so much or even fresh fish and game he caught himself. In a thousand ways, he would remind me that I was a princess — not a savage as the Chinese servants or my schoolmates said I was.

Late afternoon

We are in Cinnamon Pass. The trees are just as dense here. I can't see the sun at all. Only the green roof. But I can smell the trees from which we take the cinnamon. They grow in their own dense stands among the other trees.

When the cinnamon trees are in bloom, the mountains are scented with cinnamon, but their fragrance utterly fills the pass.

In the North, there was a forest that we called the Cinnamon Forest because there were so many of these trees. But most of them have been cut down and sent as tribute to the Chinese.

We Hsien, though, have been more careful about cutting down our land's trees. That's why the Chinese have turned to us.

At the other end of the pass, the track forks. Go north for another two days and you reach Big Rock. Go east for another half-day at a hard pace and you will reach the Chinese colony.

We could reach the colony in one day, but I can see Uncle Muntjac isn't up to it. The old warrior has been stumbling along the last few li. I should have realized how fast the others would want to travel and left him behind. And yet I know that old warrior so well now. It would have cut him as deeply as if I had taken a knife to him.

So I've ordered camp to be set up. There were complaints about that because it's dangerous with the Dog Heads about. However, I've simply ordered double sentries for the night and told them I was tired.

I can overhear the other warriors grumbling. They're sure now that their princess has been ruined by the Chinese.

Second month, seventh day
Morning

No sign of the Dog Heads. That's a relief.

We're taking a third rest near a little Chinese tea shop nine li from town. We'll make town well before sunset because we have the Chinese roads now.

Uncle and I always stop here. We're not allowed inside; but they'll serve us outside. The owner might despise us "savages" but she values our Chinese money.

The Chinese don't barter one thing for another usually. They have metal tokens that represent the value of an object. The concept is beyond some of the warriors who only know bartering.

I can hear Uncle trying to explain for the sixth time to the younger warriors what money is. When you're used to bartering, it's hard to get used to coins. Back home, if you want a chicken, you trade something useful like a fur pelt, not a lump of metal.

Uncle's been answering their questions all day. And when he doesn't know something, he makes it up. The other warriors just nod in wide-eyed innocence. I don't have the heart to correct him.

Some of the younger warriors have never been in the Chinese territory before. So everything fascinates them. I understand how they feel because I felt that way the first time I came here.

When I first left the Great Forest, I felt I had stepped

into some eerie wonder tale. Gone were the familiar wooden giants and the holy green canopy of leaves. They had been replaced by orderly rows of fruit trees and fields.

It made me angry at first because once the Great Forest covered this area and belonged to us, only to disappear forever under the colonists' axes.

And the deeper you go in the territory the more unsettling it becomes. In the Great Forest you are surrounded by shadowy creatures over whom you have no control. In fact, you are just another living thing, part of a greater chain.

However, here in the Chinese lands, humans are the most common creature. And all animals are their slaves.

Their farmsteads sit behind white plaster walls that burn in the sun. Are they prisons? Through the gates, we can see their low, one-story houses. Their roofs are also of thatch like ours, but they are flat and hard. The sides of ours curve outward in a pleasing shape like a bowl.

Their houses have little windows that stare at us like eyes. Instead of keeping the animals on the ground floor beneath the house, the Chinese keep them in separate little shacks or pens.

As soon as the younger warriors saw a small building on posts, they thought it was a Hsien house. However, it's a granary, Uncle Muntjac explained, which the Chinese build high up to keep out the rats and other animals.

He also told them that when the colonists prepare a field for the rice seedlings, they tie up a pair of poor buffalo in a harness and make them pull a thing called a plow. One man holds onto the plow while two more men pull at the heads of the buffalo. We flood our fields and send in a herd of water buffalo to let them churn up the mud.

The Chinese tie the land into a rigid pattern just like they do the buffalo — and just like they do the people. They are great counters and list-makers.

Their clothes seem strange, and they do not mark their faces or bodies. So when they die, their ghosts will wander about unknown and unloved.

It once was true that I hated the Chinese. And I wanted to run back to the Great Forest. If I were not a princess, I would have fled.

Since then, I've learned much more about the Chinese. There are even some things I admire about them. For one thing, I wish we could grow rice as tall and rich as they do. And I wish our fields could get crops like theirs do.

I can smell the noodles and meat buns. Ooo, and I think there's some of those little cakes with sesame seeds, too. Time to stop.

I've ordered another stop. I was going to make camp, but Uncle Muntjac came to me and whispered that we should go on and make the town. He can't stand to hear what the other men are saying about *his* princess.

I tried to be tactful and warn him that we would have to go fast.

Uncle Muntjac straightened proudly, and I saw a little of the warrior he had been forty years ago. He said that he would outwalk anyone when my honor was at stake.

So instead I slipped into the bushes to change my clothes. If we are going to make town today, I must be in my Chinese wardrobe. However, I will miss my skirt and roomy poncho which are so comfortable.

I would have preferred my kingfisher robe, but I knew I could not move fast enough in it. So instead, I put on a loose coat of blue silk with red cuffs on the broad sleeves. And I wore a barrel-shaped skirt of green, red, and white stripes. Around my waist, I tied an apron of black brocade decorated with yellow flowers. It's almost as comfortable as my Hsien clothes.

I'm not as happy about the matching shoes, though. It was hard to put them on after going barefoot back at home — the toes always spread a little again. Even more than the robe, though, it's important to wear the shoes. The colonists look down at anyone who goes barefoot. Even the poorest peasant will wear straw sandals.

Beyond my bushes, I can hear Uncle Muntjac taking bets that we will be able to make the colony by tonight. The others don't think I can keep up that kind of pace.

They are sure that I won't be able to walk in all my secondhand finery. My Chinese shoes will pinch my feet. (Well, they do, but not horribly). And my heavy clothing will weigh me down.

I'll show them.

The biggest worry is not whether I can make it in one day, but if he can.

Later

We're just outside of Kao-liang, the colonists' settlement.

Though he is limping, Uncle Muntjac would rather go on. However, I always have to stop by the Chinese factories.

Constant noise comes from the buildings and shacks around us. It's not like the sound of the Great Forest, though. This is not the noise of thousands of living creatures. It's metal on metal or metal on stone.

Oh, no. I've got ash on me. I must brush it off before it leaves a mark.

The ash came from a great furnace. Some men are dumping baskets of rock into it. Others work the huge box bellows, pushing it in and out so that the flames shoot from the top. And from the base of the furnace pours molten iron. Blacksmiths pound the ingots into tools and weapons. Or they cast them into all sorts of shapes.

That impresses the young warriors the most. They don't understand that there is an even more powerful factory next to the iron-makers. It's a paper factory, where men cut up linen and hemp and even old fishnets. Others mix the result with ash and then steam it. Then they pound it in a huge mortarlike bowl. It takes two men, though, to wield the "pestle," which is really a stone on a pole. Then another team stirs the resulting pulp in clean water and sets frames into it. When they take those frames out, they will be covered with white stuff. Once the sun dries it, it becomes paper.

I always stop to watch. None of the caravan can understand my fascination. They don't realize that books are mightier than any weapons that come out of the blacksmith shops.

I have to continue, though. Uncle Muntjac's giving me the eye. If he's going to win the bet, we have to leave now.

This time it was the caravan that stopped rather than Uncle Muntjac and myself. They are staring at Kao-liang.

It's here you feel the raw power of the Chinese empire. The walls of our capital are made of logs only twelve ch'ih high and none of them as thick as those that surround this town. And my village is the strongest of the tribe. Our legends talk of how the walls protected us from sieges long ago.

At first, Kao-liang's palisade had seemed like a mighty fortress since the logs had been some twenty-four ch'ih high. Now, the young warriors stare in awe at the palisade just as I did.

I don't have the heart to tell them that from what I've read in the geography books, I now realize that this town is just a little frontier outpost. And the colonists are barely holding their own against the forest. The Chinese emperors live in huge cities behind stone walls.

From the tall watchtower, a drum sounds. The newcomers grip their weapons, frightened and excited. They think the watchman is beating the alarm.

Uncle Muntjac, though, just laughs and tells them the colonist is just announcing the hour. For as the Chinese must order the land, they must do the same with time itself. They lump day and night together and split them into twelve equal parts.

Uncle Muntjac is telling the caravan to stop staring. They will see works even greater than the colony wall — palaces and towers and other magnificent structures. And they will see plenty of noble ladies in the town dressed like their princess. They must remember they are warriors and not gape like yams fresh from the dirt.

Whenever we go to the colonists' town, Uncle adopts his warrior's strut. That means that the whole pack of them will try to swagger like Uncle. I'll have to try hard not to giggle.

But now it's time to help him win his bet.

Late afternoon
Kao-liang

Heavy Chinese clothes and all, I showed the warriors that I was no soft colonial girl. And after a li or so, my feet became used to the shoes.

And for the sake of my reputation, somehow, Uncle Muntjac made it, walking as fast as warriors forty years his junior.

The real trouble was when we passed through the town gates.

The Dog Heads have been making even more trouble for the Chinese than they have been for my people. All the colonists are tense so they shoot hostile looks at us.

And none of them can tell the difference between us and Dog Heads. They can't see beyond the tattoos and the bare feet. And though the warriors are dressed in their finest ponchos and clothes and hairpins, the colonists look down their noses at them. Even a ragged beggar in a torn hemp tunic and worn straw sandals despises us.

It's just as well the caravan was too busy to notice. They were staring at the sights and sounds within the colonists' town — even Uncle Muntjac gaped like the youngest warrior, though he has seen it many times now.

I understand how they all feel. Every time I return to the colonists' town, I'm always amazed, too.

The houses here are crowded together shoulder to shoulder behind the palisade. The houses in our village are made of bamboo so that the breeze can blow through the cracks. However, the Chinese build thick walls by tamping down earth and then they cover the walls with white plaster. Because of the cramped space, the houses rise up two stories like ours. But the bottom floor is for humans to live or to work in instead of for animals.

The town is just as jammed with humans, each rushing about on his or her business. If we were not armed, I think the passersby would trample us in their hurry. There are wood choppers carrying bundles of firewood at each end of a pole, which rests on their shoulders. Or it's farmers with baskets of vegetables and fruit. Or other people with jars of oil.

Unfortunately, it was market day so the town square was jammed with people. In the shops surrounding the town square, men and women were shouting themselves hoarse. Some had jewelry to sell. Others had dead ducks and sides of pork hanging from hooks. What I like is that there are sets of weights and scales so you can be sure you're getting the right amount. It's another idea I'd like to see my people use. It would save arguments.

Within the square were stalls of cloth and bamboo where you could buy bolts of cloth or any sort of vegetable or fruit or fish. There was all sorts of grain, too. Anything a person could possibly want was for sale.

If you could not write, you could hire someone to write a letter. Or you could buy a story or a song from a performer. There were even smiles to be purchased from acrobats who did tricks there.

I stopped by a fletcher's stall where they sell Chinese arrows. The shafts of ours are of bamboo and the heads are of sharpened bone. Chinese arrows, though, are made of wood and have iron heads. They also "fletch" their arrows — that is, they fasten feathers to the end. That makes the arrows fly straighter and true.

I had a bit of Chinese money for my expenses. However, I treated all of my escort to a dozen arrows each. Uncle Muntjac told them to treat the arrows like gold.

Later
The Chen estate

I am sitting in the warehouse of Ming the trader waiting to have tea with him and Mustafa, my Arab friend.

In Ming's office are several statues of Buddhist saints and gods and goddesses. Buddhism is a religion that started in a faraway country to the east. As Ming has tried to explain to me, he tries not to harm any living thing. According to Buddhist beliefs, a person can be reborn as an animal if he or she sinned in another life. If one can avoid harming other creatures and ignoring earthly temptations, one can become pure enough to enter heaven.

Buddhism is becoming popular throughout the Chinese empire. Nobles and rich people are giving away all their land and worldly goods so that Buddhist monasteries and convents can be built.

His religion doesn't stop Ming from being a shrewd bargainer, though. I warned him about Father's decree. Ming was not happy about it at first but he said if it couldn't be helped, then he would live with it. In earlier times, such "windfall" feathers might not have gotten a very good price. However, though the kingfishers dwindle in number, the Chinese want the feathers more than ever. So we will probably get the same price that we used to get for fresh feathers.

Ming the trader is on a side street in a large windowless warehouse. It is a hot, gloomy place, but he has to keep out thieves.

Burglars can make it a rich haul if they can break into Ming's. It is bursting with rhinoceros horn and elephant tusks as well as tortoise shells. If we are not careful, those animals will disappear in our part of the Great Forest as they have in other areas.

The air is filled with camphor wood and other aromatics and edibles. And there are pearls by the bushel from the southern seas.

It is such a pleasure to see Mustafa again. He comes from a faraway country to the west and comes here to trade. Since the Chinese warlord here is at war with everyone else, he depends more and more on trade with foreigners like the Arabs.

I have learned the greeting in his tongue, and he greeted me in Chinese. He has even brought a present that he was going to leave for me. Now, though, he can give it to me in person. It is some shells of delicate red with spines.

I'll drill holes in the kindly Arab's gifts and add to the cowrie shells that decorate my belt.

In return, I gave him some of the cinnamon, which he was pleased to receive.

I asked him from where the shells came, but I did not recognize the name of the place. It is terribly frustrating not to know, but it must be far away.

It makes me realize how huge the world is. As vast as the Great Forest is, the Chinese empire is vaster. And as huge as the Chinese empire is, the world is even greater. It makes me feel small. And yet it also makes me want to be part of it now.

The more I learn, the more ignorant I realize I am. However, that only makes me eager to learn more. Learning is a hunger that only increases the more you feed it.

Uncle Muntjac is chuckling while he counts his winnings from the other warriors of the caravan — knives and assorted trinkets and notched sticks for various livestock at home.

I'm in my room in Master Chen's estate now.

After tea, I left the bargaining to the caravan leaders, for the traders have their own interpreters.

I borrowed a lantern from Ming. Then with Uncle Muntjac and six other warriors, I headed for school, which is housed in Master Chen's estate.

I was afraid one of my escort would take exception to a snooty colonist so I ordered them to keep on my heels.

Mother uses a certain tone of voice when she gives her

orders. I must have done a good imitation of it because they all nodded their heads meekly and obeyed.

I think they would have stayed close to me, anyway, because everything was so new. And whatever the Chinese might think of us, they have a healthy respect for the sharpness of our swords and arrows.

Master Chen's ancestor must have been longing for home when he was exiled here. For he built an estate like the one he had in the North. It's four sets of buildings surrounded by a wall and split into two halves. There is only one opening, a gate near the southwest corner.

Chou the gatekeeper scowled at me like he usually does. And when he saw even more of my people, the scowl only grew worse. The first time I came to this school, that look had very nearly made me turn around and run. I had to remind myself that I was a princess of the Hsien.

Chou blocked us, saying that he couldn't allow so many painted buffalo inside.

I told him that these were my royal escort and should be treated with respect.

He answered that I might call myself a princess, and I might wear his mistress's cast-off robe, but I was only a tattooed savage at heart. And my palace was only a big stable.

I felt like slapping him. However, I remembered that I was an ambassador in my own small way.

So with the greatest dignity I could muster, I replied

that whether they would be allowed to stay or not was up to his master and not to him.

He didn't get out of the way but just snarled an insult that isn't suitable for me to record here.

Uncle Muntjac may not know Chinese, but he could understand the tone and the expression.

So he drew his knife. And right then and there he would have slit the gatekeeper's throat.

I grabbed his arm and commanded him to stop. We were not in the Great Forest. We were Master Chen's guests, and he might not like it if we made a mess in his nice, clean courtyard.

Uncle Muntjac looked disappointed but Chou grew very pale. I told him to go to the kitchen and get a meal together for my warriors. Chou had the good sense to use that as an excuse to hide. He bolted inside so fast that he left a sandal behind.

We had no way of warning Master Chen in advance that I would be bringing a larger escort, but I thought he would find room for them.

I led them through the wide courtyard where there were only a few shade trees and a well.

A second gate let us into a larger courtyard surrounded by two-story buildings on three sides. Lanterns as big as melons hung everywhere giving light. At the rear is a huge reception hall for official business and banquets.

Master Chen has his study on the left while the school is housed in rooms in the buildings on the right.

The roofs here are of heavy tiles. The end tiles have guardian animals and creatures. The windows are large and of carved wood. Everywhere you look there's something to delight the eye.

Along the sides are verandas. Tile roofs cover them and rest upon large red wooden pillars with carved animals curling around their tops and bottoms.

A hallway that passes through the school allows you into the right half of the complex where the servants and livestock live in small buildings and sheds. Cooking is also done in the kitchen.

Chou was nowhere to be seen there, but he had already passed on my request. The kitchen was bustling, getting ready for the evening meal. The head chef, Chi, was steaming dumplings and other snacks for my escort.

I thanked him for his recipes and told him how popular the dishes were at home. He raised his eyebrows skeptically, but he was polite enough not to wonder out loud what Hsien would know about Chinese food.

I suppose I shouldn't have worried because Uncle Muntjac and Chi are old friends. They hit it off when Uncle Muntjac began hunting outside of town and providing wild game for the Chens' larder.

Chi was delighted by the prospect of having more

hunters. He said there were a couple of sheds that were empty. He'd make sure that Wu the Steward understood and that mats would be put inside so that my escort would be comfortable.

Then I went back through the school, crossed the courtyard, and passed through the reception hall into the private quarters of Master Chen, the last set of two-story buildings behind the reception hall. In the center of this small complex is a garden. Master Chen and his family live in the buildings surrounding it on three sides.

It's strange, but I've come to think of this place as a second home. I have a lovely room that lets me look out at the garden. Even when the Chinese allow a bit of nature into their lives, it must be orderly. Both the trees and flowers. I'm surprised they haven't set up a schedule for the birds to sing.

I have cabinets for my clothes and even my own Chinese bed so I don't sleep on the floor. There are six short legs, each as long as my hand. The wooden bed frame is surrounded by a low lattice of bamboo around which red silk has been wound and ornamented with bronze. Then slats of wood have been laid across the frame itself to form a platform for a mat upon which I sleep. I have a ceramic headrest in the shape of a sleeping girl, but I prefer to sleep without it as I would back at Kingfisher Hill.

Four poles rise from each corner of the bed to a frame

above me. Covering the frame and hanging down the sides is gauzy green silk. The design is of trees with birds singing and deer galloping. (I think it's the Chinese idea of what the Great Forest looks like.) I like to sit on my bed and pull the curtains down so that I am surrounded by green light once again.

In one corner of the bed is a small bronze censer in the shape of twelve sacred mountains with fantastical creatures on it. The Chinese believe there are certain ill humors in the air that cause illnesses — like malaria. So they burn certain herbs in the censer to drive away the humors and keep disease at bay. I don't bother using it because the air doesn't seem to bother me. However, Chinese who are new to Kao-liang often get sick and even die.

I also have a lovely table of reddish-brown hardwood the same length and height as the bed platform. I can use it both for dining or writing. The legs are thin and curve into rails that rest on the floor.

At night I can read or write by the light of fat Chinese candles with reed wicks.

Still, I like my home at Kingfisher Hill. A bamboo house has spaces that let it breathe. Chinese houses are so shut up.

I —

What's all that noise? Has a buffalo herd gotten loose?

It was my guard!

They came looking for me, which caused an uproar among Master Chen's servants.

The problem is that I stay in the women's quarters in the last set of two-story buildings behind the reception hall. Until now, Uncle Muntjac had always been content to stay with the servants in the right half of the complex. But when he remembered my parents had told the guard not to let me out of their sight, he and the other warriors searched all over the estate for me. The trouble is that strange men are not allowed into this part of the family quarters.

Wu the steward is a little man but he acts like he's ten ch'ih tall. And he has a haughty stare that cuts you down to mouse size. I have managed to make a compromise between him and my guards. One of them will be allowed to stand watch in the reception hall where he can keep an eye on my room on the second floor.

Wait. Who's going to keep an eye on them? I'm going to tell them in no uncertain terms that they are not to leave the estate short of fire or flood.

I am not about to turn six Hsien warriors loose in the town. We have enough trouble with the Dog Heads. We do not need to start a second war with the colonists.

Sometimes it's hard to tell who's escorting whom.

I feel better after a night's sleep and washing up. I —

That was Madame's maid, Mei. She always looks at me as if I smell terrible.

Madame has summoned me.

My hair! My clothes! I need to do a dozen things to make myself presentable.

And even then that probably won't be enough.

But there's no time!

I hate the way I sound. But Madame is Madame.

No, I shouldn't write things like that. She has been kind to me in so many ways. She could have assigned me to a dingy room in the servants' quarters, but she has treated me like family. And she has given me many clothes and other things. I shouldn't be ungrateful.

Madame is Master Chen's daughter-in-law. She and her two daughters live with me in the women's quarters while Master Chen lives in his.

Madame's son, Lin, lives in the building on the right with a family of distant cousins — a father and mother and two more boys, both of whom are younger than Lin.

Master Chen might be the head of the household. However, it is Madame who runs things.

And she wants to see me immediately. I'm sure it's to inspect me.

Madame was downstairs in the large room she uses for weaving. The place was blazing with lanterns and candles so she could work.

The Chinese make silk from the cocoons of silkworms. I have watched the Sung servants feed them leaves from the mulberry trees that they buy from the farmers. When the silkworms have spun their cocoons, they are killed, the cocoons are boiled, and the fibers are unwound and removed. The skeins of raw silk are then dyed and wound onto reels.

Her two daughters were there, too. Ch'ai, who is four years older than me, simply nodded. She tolerates me.

Ch'ai was dressed in a robe of brown silk with flowers and jujubes sewn in a design of red thread. Her hair was swept to either side like bird wings. She's sweet-tempered and almost as placid as a cow.

Yü is a year younger than me, but she's tart as a green persimmon. She scowled when she saw me. "So you're back, Leather Foot."

Yü had named me Leather Foot on the day we met because my feet, in contrast to hers, were so tough.

She has made it clear that she hates "savages." Though Ch'ai has never begrudged me the outfits she has given me, her little sister has often sneered that I sometimes wear clothes she had discarded for rags.

Yü prides herself on being so modern. She complains that it is hard to keep up with current fashions in the middle of nowhere. Her rose-colored robe was covered with curlicues and geometric patterns sewn in silver thread. I knew the design must be of expensive Persian silk. Yü had more expensive clothes than her mother or sister.

I stood waiting patiently for Madame to finish. She weaves some intricate designs of silk and does much of the sewing herself. With one chore or another, she is often the first person up and the last to go to bed. I could really admire her — if she did not frighten me so.

From what I have read, Madame is a woman of old-fashioned virtues. Quiet, hard-working, and efficient. Certainly her two daughters are not like her.

Both of them were supposed to be darning clothes, but Ch'ai just sat there staring through a window at the moonlit garden, probably daydreaming about her betrothed again.

She had been going to her father's school, too, and her husband-to-be was perfectly willing to have a learned

wife. However, it was her future father-in-law who forbade any more lessons. He quoted an old proverb. "A stupid woman is a virtuous woman."

It seems that Master Chen has scandalized the town by actually educating his own granddaughters. And of course, now he has accepted not only another female student, but a "savage" at that.

Everyone in the family wanted Ch'ai to end the engagement, but Ch'ai is so in love with her intended that she simply quit going to school. She has filled an entire room with chests and baskets full of clothes and other things she will need when she moves in with her husband.

I find it hard to see how she can be in love with a boy whom she's only met a few brief times — and then only with chaperones. And I also don't see what kind of life she's going to lead with her in-laws. Once she's married, she'll be expected to obey them absolutely.

If that's love, I don't want it. (Note to myself: Kumquat has a lot of philters and charms to make people fall in love. I wonder if she has one to prevent that awful disease?)

Though the younger daughter, Yü, also had some darning on her lap, she was studying her image in Madame's antique hand mirror and trying her curls in different places.

The mirror was usually in Madame's bedroom. It's one of those marvels of the Chinese. One side is polished bronze and the other side has a pattern of phoenixes.

I understand that Yü had also attended the school one time. However, she quit before I started taking classes. It can't be a question of intelligence. She's certainly smart enough. Now she spends most of her time playing games or arranging flowers or visiting her friends — all of them daughters of other rich families.

Madame's hair and clothes are always perfect. Today, she had wound her hair around a wire frame of butterfly wings. Madame's tresses seemed to hover magically. Pearls had been attached and they gleamed like magical moons as she moved her head. And though she works at her loom, there is not a strand of hair out of place.

Pinning the assemblage of hair in the back of her head was a kingfisher hairpin. The bright blue feathers gleamed within the blackness and contrasted nicely with her robe of red silk with black silk cuffs.

One thing, though, always puzzles me. As rich as the Chen women are, they always wear such tiny earrings. They're certainly pretty enough — of pearls or gold or jewels. However, they're never longer than a little finger. It's a wonder they don't lose them all the time.

When she finally finished, Madame turned to me. If I hadn't been the target, I think I would have found it amusing. Her face was such a study when she saw me.

"Oh, dear," she said. "Oh, dear."

It's not that Madame hits me with a stick or scolds me.

It's just that she makes me feel so loud and crude compared to her. I didn't know what to make of this soft-spoken lady, and I'm sure she doesn't know what to make of me.

When I first came into the Chen household, all the rules felt as tight and stuffy as the clothes. However, I've come to see that they have their own value, even if everything is so different from how I was raised.

I made my polite greetings and apologized for coming back so early.

When Madame speaks to me, I have noticed a slight delay that is not there in her conversations with other people. It's as if she always has to think twice about her words to me.

She murmured back politely that I was welcome back anytime. However, she was surprised at what the sun had done to my complexion in that short time. I had obviously not been using the hat she had given me before I left for Kingfisher Hill.

It had been a broad-brimmed straw hat with a silk veil.

Yü was more blunt. She said I was as tanned as a field hand.

I said that I had forgotten the hat — though, to be honest, I simply had not packed it. When I had worn it, I had felt as if I had stuck my head inside a basket.

Personally, I see nothing wrong with having dark skin. However, Chinese women like Madame pride themselves on not having to work in the fields. When Madame putters about in the garden, she drapes herself in clothes and a hat and veil so that she looks like some ghost among the flowers.

Ch'ai, though, said she would give me some cosmetics. I think sometimes she considers me a pet whom she has taught to do tricks.

Madame added that it was important for everyone in the household to look their best. And she motioned for me to sit down.

I didn't stop to think. When I sat down on the mat, I stuck out my legs in front of me as I would at home.

Yü always looked for a way to insult me. "Leather Foot's gone back to sitting like a winnowing basket again!"

I hadn't understood that comment until I saw a Chinese winnowing basket. It's low and flat so it spreads out.

Instantly, I pulled my legs underneath me the way a proper Chinese should.

However, Madame simply said that perhaps I need a refresher course after my visit home.

I must be careful of things like that when I am at school. Sometimes I feel as if everyone is watching me, waiting for a chance to sneer at the "savage." I feel so self-conscious here.

Madame must have seen in my face how I felt. She called to Yü to bring over the mirror. She's given it to me!

Yü protested that it was an antique.

Madame, though, says that it's become a bit dingy with age. Even so, perhaps it will be of some small use to me. She had been intending to give it to me before I left last time.

Yü got very angry at that. She wanted to know how her mother could give something so precious to a savage who sleeps with pigs.

As I cradled the mirror, I told Yü that my bedroom was over the pigs, not with them. And I added that the Chinese word for family was a picture of a pig near a house. So she could hardly talk.

I felt very bad that I said anything at all and apologized to Madame right away.

However, Madame simply smiled and said it just showed that everyone enjoyed a bit of pork. Some of us more than others.

I just don't know what to make of Madame. Sometimes she can be so generous — as with the antique mirror. And yet other times she can make me feel so small. Every day I feel as if I fail her daily quizzes.

I'm going to do my best to dress myself properly for supper. Ch'ai has sent me a white foundation cosmetic. It's a little white cake molded like a flower. It's almost too pretty to use, though.

What am I to do? Madame and Yü have made it clear

that they think I am too dark — and too tattooed. They are my hosts after all.

And yet if I do what they want, I will act as if I am ashamed of being a Hsien.

Perhaps if I try a bit . . .

Ugh! I hate how it feels.

They'll have to be satisfied if I wash up, do my hair, and put on a good robe.

It's really my life, I suppose. They want me to use Chinese paint on my Hsien's skin.

Sometimes I feel as if I am like one of those Chinese acrobats I saw at a temple festival. I balance high in the air upon one hand.

It makes me feel so dizzy and tired.

Afternoon

Master Chen has still not come home yet. He is meeting with the magistrate and other important people.

Now that the garrison has been withdrawn, there are only civilian volunteers and a few retired veterans to protect the colony. They have formed a militia. I have watched them practice their style of warfare. They march about in formation. However, since they wear everyday clothes, they seem as if they are rehearsing for a dance festival.

Certainly the Dog Heads aren't afraid of the town's militia. They have been attacking the Chinese as often as they have been assaulting us.

It seems I can't escape talk of war wherever I go.

The walls of the Chens' dining room are of carved wooden panels. The one that fascinates me the most is of a garden in the snow, which I have never seen. Red pillars rise from the floor. Their tops and the beams are carved with scenes from the Chinese heaven. And the bottoms of the pillars are decorated with sea creatures. Overhead, the rain had begun again. I could hear it pounding on the roof tiles.

As soon as I came in, Ch'ai was worried that I hadn't liked the white cake foundation. However, I said that it had made my skin burn. I thought it might give me a rash.

With a sigh, Madame said that my face should grow pale if I stayed indoors for a while. And since I loved books so much, that's probably what would happen.

Yü made the snide comment that they would just have to hide me from any visitors until my flesh "lightened" a bit.

I'm sure that beneath my tanned skin my cheeks were burning a bright red.

Ch'ai tried to make up for her little sister by complimenting me on my robe and hair, which I had put up in buns on either side of my head.

Yü agreed, saying that my hairstyle and robe never went out of fashion — no matter how old they were. (My kingfisher robe is an old one that Madame had taken from a chest and given to me.)

My parents would have been proud, though. I didn't let Yü goad me into a fight. Just as the Big Rock folk never goad my father into a quarrel.

However, Yü made me more determined than ever to be a proper Chinese lady — at least for one evening. I made sure to sit with my legs tucked underneath me this time. (Since I hadn't been in that posture for a while, my legs are still aching.)

We each sat on a small, low platform. Madame had a lovely armrest made of ebony and inlaid with ivory that pictured partridges in a field of flowers. And behind her was a tall screen of cherry trees in blossom.

On two sides of each platform were portable screens with different scenes. They protected against drafts and even gave a small degree of privacy.

In front of each platform was a low table. Large bronze serving vessels and jars stood to the side from which servants filled our bowls. Madame's maid, Mei, supervised the service with a vigilant eye.

The first course was of paper-thin slices of fish in a light sauce of scallions and ginger.

After many embarrassing lessons — and much taunting from Yü — I finally mastered chopsticks. It was either learn or starve. The Chinese frown on eating with your bare hands as much as they despise bare feet.

I made sure to take small bites and not to drip or spill. I wanted to show Madame that she did not have to give me a remedial lesson on everything.

The rest of the courses followed rapidly. There was duck and beef and chicken. When Madame was finished with each dish, she would set her chopsticks down over her rice bowl as a signal to the servants to bring the next one. Since Madame sometimes only tasted a dish, I sometimes got no more than a nibble. My favorite was the chicken in peony sauce so I ate with bigger bites and a bit more quickly than I should have.

The food, though, wouldn't go to waste. Down in the kitchen the servants would be feasting.

Madame made a point of talking to me about the current songs and dances and the latest fine points in arranging flowers. And Ch'ai told me about the latest fashion in cosmetics, hairstyles, and clothes. Everyone seems to want northern-style patterns of snowy mountains and sheep. The both of them seem to think such information is as important as anything in my books.

When I first came here, I despised Madame and her

daughters for their confined, protected way of life. (So perhaps my feud with Yü is partly my fault.) I thought they were simply idle flowers in the garden.

However, the more time I spent with Madame, I realized how busy she was. I've come to see that she has her own quiet strengths. She is like the river at home. It might look calm on the surface but beneath, its currents flow deep and powerful.

And even if I cannot see spending all my time their way, I appreciate the fact that Madame and Ch'ai have tried to include me in their activities. In Ch'ai's way of thinking, the cosmetic advice was not an insult but an attempt to help me the way she would want to be helped.

Yü, though, is another matter. She nips, she bites, she stings at every opportunity.

It started out innocently enough when Lin came in. He is Madame's son and Master Chen's heir. He's about my age but swaggers around worse than Little Tiger. He's bright and handsome and wealthy. Everyone, including Master Chen, spoils him.

His long hair had been twisted artfully with blue silk ribbons into narrow braids that swept around the sides of his head, rose up the back, and were gathered in a knot at the top. Hairpins with large pearls had been used to fasten the braids and knots. The Chinese, though, don't have big topknots as do the Hsien.

Lin was wearing a robe of blue silk embroidered with lucky symbols in gold thread. The Chen family would never be mistaken for peasants.

"So you're back," he grunted in greeting to me and dropped down on his mother's platform. "Good. Grandfather won't be able to call on me as much."

Casually, he began helping himself with his fingers to things from his mother's bowl. And Madame did not complain. Instead she signed to a maid who raised the lid on a bronze bowl so Madame could use her chopsticks to select especially choice morsels for her son.

As it turned out, he'd already eaten with his male cousins, but he had come to see if we had anything better.

His sisters teased him for a bit about being a greedy pig while his mother defended him, saying that he was a growing boy.

When Lin was done, we finished the meal with some fresh fruit for dessert.

And then it was time for the entertainment. Ch'ai and Yü did the same dance that I had done back home, but they did it so much better. It puts me to shame.

I tried to sing a little ballad, but was so nervous I was unable to keep in tune for most of it. Fortunately, Madame joined me halfway through, and I clung to her clear soprano like a drowning girl holds onto a log.

Ch'ai was polite enough to smile, but Yü and Lin

teased me mercilessly. And then Lin did a little comic dance he had seen in some show. His legs and arms became all loose as if they were made of bean curd.

Now that we had all taken a turn, we began to debate on what to do next for our amusement. And Lin suggested we play the popular game of "sixes," which he offered to teach me.

Madame frowned, saying that it was a game for the men and not ladies.

Ch'ai, though, said it was fun. She had played it just last week when she had visited the magistrate's house.

If it had been anyone else but Lin suggesting the game, Madame would still have refused. However, I've noticed that the Chinese favor the boys just like my own people do.

And so Madame sent her maid, Mei, to fetch the set.

Sixes is played on a board and gets its name from the six bamboo sticks that are used. Each stick has different markings and is put into a cup. A player shakes the cup and then dumps the sticks out. Then, depending on how they land, you move your piece around the board.

Lin, though, must be crazy about the game because he had bought a small table with the board built into the top. It's a lovely table with horse-hoof legs, and the pieces are of the animals of the four directions. The white tiger is for the west, the green dragon for the east, the black tortoise for the north, and the redbird for the south.

Lin chose the dragon, and I chose the bird.

The rules were simple enough, and I could have beaten Lin. I had played games with him before — like chess or stones — and I quickly learned not to beat him. Lin was a gracious winner but a terrible loser. And I didn't want him pouting or throwing a tantrum and spoiling what was a generally pleasant evening.

Even Madame and Yü wound up learning the game.

So, when it was my turn to play, I was careful to lose, though I could have won most of the time.

Then Yü said that to make it proper fun we had to wager something. I thought the wager would be some chore or a few small coins. No! She wanted the mirror!

At first, Madame was against it, but Lin tapped the jade clasp that holds his belt together. It was in the shape of a tiger's head and is lovely work. He said he would back my wager.

I gave him a startled look. He knew that I had been losing on purpose! Master Chen's grandson is no dull, drowsy lizard.

Since it was her son's wish, Madame was silent. Even so, I didn't want to risk my mirror, but Yü kept goading me.

She made me so angry that I lost my judgment and agreed.

Ch'ai asked what Yü would have to give up if I won. I would have settled for a scarf, but Lin said what would he want with a girl's scarf?

Madame mentioned the entertainment at the Sung estate tomorrow night. Yü would have to take me if she lost.

With a mischievous grin, Lin said that would be fine but with one further forfeit: Yü must carry me on her back to the temple and then home again.

Yü was so confident that she happily promised.

When her first throw was a good one, Yü started beaming. She could already see the mirror in her room and the jade dragon on her belt.

However, it was as if I had saved up all my luck for the evening. Soon, all the throws were going my way while she kept getting one terrible throw after another. By the time I won, she was almost in tears.

I felt so sorry for her that I said it would be enough to take us to the temple. However, pride runs strong in all of Master Chen's family. A wager was a wager, Yü insisted.

I bet she'll pinch me all the way there and back.

My first day back at school.

There are a half dozen of us gathered in the large room. Decorating the walls are strips of paper with poems written in Master Chen's elegant hand, and plaques with different virtuous mottoes like: To Study Hard Is Glorious!

When class begins, Master Chen will sit upon a platform against one wall. His red silk cushion waits for him to sit down, and there is a curving armrest carved in the shape of a dragon. It's made of some dark red wood with purplish streaks.

We students sit on mats in perpendicular rows on either side of the platform. Lin and his cousins sit in the left row. I sit in the right row with two younger boys, both of them from families of rich neighbors of the Chens.

Before each row is a long, low table. Lin and his older cousins have unrolled a scroll that covers the whole table. They are studying the great classics of China. The scroll is full of complicated, obscure Chinese characters and sentences that are hard to understand. Because it's an important book, it's been written on silk.

Master Chen says the first books were written on strips of bamboo that were tied together. Over the centuries, though, they have been copied and recopied on different materials. Now most books are copied onto scrolls of paper — made by gluing pieces together.

When we had first arrived, Master Chen greeted me warmly and asked how the Spring Festival had been, but I had to tell him it had been canceled. I think he would have liked to have asked me more, but I am wary of reminding the rest of the school that I am a Hsien. They already tease me enough as it is.

I study with the younger students. Most of the time we study word lists that are copied on cheap, coarse paper. So we just unroll it on the floor in front of the table and then lean over to memorize and copy.

The word lists are different categories of synonyms. Today, I guess we're going to work on all the different words for "house."

I've got my sheets of paper laid out in front of me. They may be coarse and cheap, but they are still precious to me. And I have my brush and my ink jar. (It's in the shape of a frog.)

I'm all ready to start.

What a lovely morning after yesterday's rain! Warm. Sunny.

I can see bits of dust dancing in a shaft of sunlight. They whirl and spin. It's how I feel inside.

Lin is already bored, though. He's far too clever for the rest of us, and so he's usually way ahead of the lessons. Unfortunately, he sets a bad example for the other boys.

Lin is bragging about a kite he purchased last afternoon.

I have to stop now. I hear Master Chen's footsteps.

Later

Master Chen has taken my homework into his study to look at it. Lin's grandfather was barely gone before he and the other boys slipped outside to fly a kite.

Lin even invited me, surprising the other boys as well as me. However, if Master Chen was brave and generous enough to take me on as a student, I won't repay him by playing the truant.

That afternoon

Master Chen looked so sad when he came back and found the schoolroom empty. He is a tall man with large bags under his eyes and a long chin. It makes him look like a sad, tired dog.

Covering his topknot is a black cap of cloth that always seems about to fall off.

I offered to fetch the other students so he could begin lessons.

He said, "Don't bother, Princess Redbird."

Princess Redbird was my school name. The Chinese have several names besides their personal names. I was named Redbird not only for the color of my clothes but also because the Redbird is the Chinese symbol of the south.

He told me that none of the town children valued what he had to pass on. Not even his grandson. Only I did.

Before I could feel good, though, he said this was the first time I had failed in my homework.

I complained that I didn't see why he wanted me to write a history of his homeland when he already had a library full of books about the Chinese empire.

He said that I had misheard him. He had asked for a history of *our* homeland. And that included the Great Forest as well as the colonists' holdings. So that meant the Hsien as well as the Chinese.

I warned him that he might not like what a Hsien had to write.

He said that was exactly what he wanted — the point of view of the Hsien as well as the other tribes in the Great Forest. Only then could the history of our homeland be complete.

That's what makes Master Chen so unusual. Most of the Chinese think the free tribes are lower than bugs. From what I've heard in the town, the other Chinese colonists think he's a little odd. Chen is as unusual for a Chinese as Father is for a Hsien.

So I reluctantly got out my diary. It was the scraps of paper that I had pasted together into a scroll.

I expected him to get mad because of the things I had written about his people.

Worse, I thought he might even exile me from his wonderful library. And that really scared me.

However, when he began to read he just smiled and said that this was more what he had in mind. Later, as Master Chen and I spoke, I was still puzzled. Why, I asked him, wasn't he angry about what I had said about the Chinese?

He answered that it was because what I said was true. And though the Chinese looked upon the forest folk as barbarians, the Chinese had acted just as barbaric. One day we would all realize we were the same people.

I said I could see why Master Chen's ancestor was exiled here if he thought like his descendant and said so.

With a laugh, he told me that his ancestor had been a follower of an ancient Confucian philosopher called Master Meng who lived in times almost as perilous as ours.

Master Meng taught what true civilization was. Humans were good at heart and so kindness will drown cruelty just as water will put out a fire.

I said that I hadn't seen many examples of it in his history books. I repeated what Little Tiger had said: The Chinese peace was bought at the expense of their enemies.

Master Chen nodded his head. Unfortunately, not even his people were as civilized as they should be. And for the last three centuries, more people had been reading books of warfare than Master Meng's books.

For all his book learning, Master Chen is not very practical. And yet I think he has many ideas with which Father would agree.

Normally, I would resent any assignments that took away the time to read the stories.

But I'll have to read more of this Master Meng so I can tell Father.

At least, Master Chen says I don't have to imitate the great historians in his library. The most important history books began when someone recorded personal moments. From small things come big things. From small facts come big books. So I should just keep writing down whatever I think.

I guess I should be flattered.

But I smell more schoolwork.

I think Master Chen can be sneaky in his own polite way.

I must stop now. I have to get ready for the entertainment tonight at the Sungs'. I have been to some performances at the Buddhist temples. The priests put them on to draw people in and then teach them about the Buddhist religion. My teacher does not approve of the new religion from India. However, he lets us go to the shows. They're quite spectacular with sword swallowers and fire-eaters and all sorts of dances. Sometimes the dancers act out stories from the life of Buddha. Other times they dress up as animals and perform a dance that tells some of the Buddhist animal fables.

However, tonight should be different. The Sungs are the richest family in the colony. They have their own orchestra and dancers and will be performing dances that tell stories from Chinese history and legends.

In honor of the occasion, I have decided to wear the plum robe, and put up my hair in the Chinese fashion.

That night

I had better write down some notes since this has become an assignment.

Madame hired a carriage to take us to the Sung estate. It was a big box on two huge wheels pulled by a pair of horses. The compartment was big enough for Madame, her children, and myself.

Lin, of course, reminded us of the bet. Yü said she was not about to carry me all the way to the Sungs' who lived several li outside of town. I was simply happy to be going, so I said that I could walk on my own two feet. (On festivals, plays were performed at various temples in the town, and I had been to them.)

However, Lin appealed to his mother, and as always she gave in to him. It was decided that I would walk until I reached the outer courtyard where the carriage waited. There Yü would carry me from the inner gate to the carriage.

And when we arrived at the Sungs', she would carry me to the nearest gate or fifty paces — whichever came first.

A servant led the way with a lit lantern. It was a round paper globe on which the word for truth had been painted. I recognized Master Chen's hand.

It seemed like a magical night. The air, though warm, was dry for once. Tiny frogs in the garden were making little chirping noises. And everyone, even Yü, seemed to be in a good mood.

The windows of Master Chen's study were lit by lanterns and candles. As always, he must be reading. He liked to say that a true teacher was a student who never stopped learning. However, he came out long enough to wish us a pleasant evening — and to assign an essay about what Lin and I saw tonight.

When we got to the gate opening onto the courtyard,

Yü squatted down. I was very careful as I climbed onto her back, winding my arms around her neck. Warning me not to disturb her hair, she clasped my legs and then stood up.

I had expected her to pinch me or even drop me. However, she carried me out into the lantern-lit courtyard. Chou stood by the outer gate. His jaw dropped when he saw his mistress carrying me.

Though snug for the five of us, Madame had seen to it that the carriage was furnished with silk cushions and snacks.

I settled in comfortably and looked out the carriage door at Uncle Muntjac who had been dutifully trailing us. I told him not to get into trouble while I was gone.

However, Uncle Muntjac insisted upon going along. Six shadows left a corner of the courtyard where they had been waiting. And then they fell in behind the carriage.

I was terribly embarrassed. Yü threw a tantrum. Even Madame was upset, saying there wasn't time to hire another carriage. The only one who seemed to be enjoying himself was Lin.

I argued with Uncle Muntjac but his mind was set. He had his orders and he wasn't going to let me out of his sight — especially since I was going outside the walls. They didn't need a carriage since they had their legs. It would be a sad day when a warrior of the Hsien could not keep up with a plodding Chinese carriage.

Perhaps the younger warriors could, but I had my doubts about Uncle Muntjac. However, I couldn't change the mind of that proud, old, stubborn warrior.

So we set off. Fortunately, the large carriage could not go very fast. I kept peeking through the window, but my guard jogged along easily. And though Uncle Muntjac was limping, he stayed with us.

The fields stretched away on either side, all newly plowed. I love the smell of the fresh-turned earth. It's so full of promise and hope.

However, Yü complained about the stink and began to fan herself vigorously. She kept it up even as we passed through large orchards whose blossoms scented the air. The fruit trees looked all puffy and silvery in the moonlight.

The workers on the estate live in a small village not too far away from the Sung mansion.

It was about three li to the Sung estate. It's huge! Their holdings stretched as far as I could see in the moonlight. I had thought Master Chen's estate was big, but theirs would include three of his. And the buildings and walls are more ornate. There is gold paint everywhere. It was almost too much.

When the carriage stopped in the outer courtyard, Yü told me to wait and then got out first. Bending over, she told me to hop onto her back.

Our host and some of his family had come out to greet us. I told her again that it wasn't necessary, but she was resolute that she would pay her forfeit.

Some eyebrows rose on our hosts' faces as Yü carried me toward the gate leading to the inner courtyard. Lin didn't help any by skipping in front and pretending to lead Yü by a halter.

I knew how proud Yü was. She must have been dying inside. So I whispered to her to put me down. She had paid me already.

When I tried to slide off, she gripped my legs tightly. She insisted that no one would accuse her of cheating on a bet. (But this would teach her to gamble with me.)

One of the Sung boys was Lin's age. He greeted Lin and then stared at me with wide eyes. "Is that a savage?"

Yü snapped that I was a princess in my own right. The boy must have known Yü because he became quite polite. No wise person undertakes a fight with Yü if he or she can help it.

The boy asked me if I lived in the Great Forest with all the wild beasts and monsters.

Yü answered for me, saying that I had left my pet tigers back at their home. But they would come at my call so he should be careful. And the boy backed away as if I were on fire.

When Yü set me down in the next courtyard, we shared a giggle together. Then I asked her why she had defended me.

As she straightened her clothes, she said that I might be a savage, but I was also a guest. And no outsider could insult a guest of theirs.

"Only insiders?" I asked her.

"Exactly," she said, dusting off her hands.

Because it was a clear night, the entertainment was to be held outside. Platforms and cushions had been set up and there were tables with refreshments in front. And a small army of servants to keep serving drinks and new delicacies.

The Sungs themselves are a large clan. I didn't sort out all the names and relationships. However, they were all sumptuously dressed in silk with lovely patterns in gold thread. And the colors! I felt as if a flock of exotic birds had landed about me.

The men and boys wore jade belt clasps and even the counterweights for their purses were of jade. I know enough of Chinese design to know that the carving is antique. The women and girls wear their hair around fanciful wire frames. Pearls and jewels decorate their tresses.

There were several girls my age and everyone was making sure that Lin chatted with them. Every time Lin tried to talk to someone else, Madame steered him back to the Sung girls. So I think there's some matchmaking underway.

I think both the Chens and Sungs are hoping Lin will become interested. I can see why Madame wants Lin to marry a Sung girl.

For the evening the Sungs hired some other performers as well. There was a lion dance and then acrobats who tumbled all about and twisted their bodies in all sorts of shapes. There was also a splendid dance where they acted out a story about a man who tried to kill an emperor.

I felt a nudge. It was Uncle Muntjac who had crept over and wanted to know what was happening. The rest of my escort knelt behind him. It was quite improper for servants to sit with the guests, and there were many startled, angry looks from both the Sungs and the Chens — except for Lin who was grinning from ear to ear. Yü glared at me. "Tell them to go away," she whispered.

I was embarrassed. But Uncle Muntjac and the others were as curious and excited as small boys at a wrestling match. I couldn't dismiss them.

"You're always talking about how superior the Chinese are," I told her. "You should be happy my warriors like your dances."

Madame begged the Sungs to indulge us. I guess the

Sungs must really want the match because they gave in when Lin asked. They even told the dancers to start over.

So I explained the story to my warriors who watched with open mouths as the dancers fought their duel. They were very clever how they used scarves to imitate swords during the combat.

Ch'ai made a point of whispering to me, "Do you see how important a woman's accessories are?"

I promised to treat my scarf with more respect.

The next story-dance told the tale of a young man who avenges his father's death. I got so caught up in the entertainment that I quite forgot my guard. The dancer playing the young man wore a robe of all white, which is the color Chinese wear when they mourn. He began a sad song of how a tiger had killed his father, and left the body on a mountain. He was going to go up and bring his father home and perhaps avenge himself upon the tiger.

He acted out the ascent of the mountain in song and dance, clambering over rocks and through the dense forest that covered the mountain.

It's strange, but the forest of the dance was quite different from the one that I know. It was full of monsters and awful beasts just as the Sung boy had thought. I think most Chinese believe anything beyond their orderly little farms is a place full of demons and monsters. And the

Great Forest, with its tangle of trees and bushes and vines, is an even more fearsome place.

So the hero had a hard time of it. It took him a while to find his father's tracks, and then he found his father's bones. He wept for his father, remembering all the wonderful times they had and what sacrifices his father had made for him. It was a song so mournful that it almost made me cry, too.

Then, just when he was about to gather the bones and take them back for burial, the tiger danced out of the forest. It was only a dancer in costume, but he moved just like one. Slowly, he stalked the hero who wasn't aware of the tiger. I held my breath as the tiger got ready to pounce.

Suddenly, from behind me I heard someone shout a warning. It was the younger warriors. This was their first time in the colony so they had never seen such a thing before and thought the tiger was real. Or perhaps they thought the dancer was one of those man-tigers like in the stories back home.

Drawing their knives, my guard gallantly rushed to the rescue.

Fortunately, Uncle Muntjac and I were able to stop them before they skewered the poor dancer playing the tiger. When I sat back down, my cheeks felt as hot as a stove's sides. At that moment, I wouldn't have had to borrow any of Ch'ai's rouge to redden them.

Lin, though, jumped to his feet and said he hoped the Sungs had enjoyed our own little performance. It was a flimsy enough excuse and everyone knew it was a lie. However, the Chinese have a concept called "face" and Lin was trying to save mine.

Because it was Lin saying it, everyone simply laughed and said it was a good joke on them. The dance went on to its finish in which the hero killed the tiger to cheers from my guard. I should say, though, the tiger didn't seem to have the same energy. He was too busy glancing nervously at my guard, ready to turn and run if they came after him.

All in all, it was a satisfying evening.

Yü insisted on carrying me through the outer courtyard to the carriage again. Once more, I tried to refuse, but she told me not to be tiresome. She intended to keep her word.

I wish she was a friend rather than an enemy. Of all the Chens, I think she is the strongest.

On the way home in the carriage, Lin whispered to me to get my essay to him early next morning so he could copy it. He would change enough words so his grandfather would not suspect. He is always copying my homework and acting as if he is doing me a favor. However, because of what he had done at the performance, I gave in.

We were about a li from the Sungs when we heard distant gongs sounding out an alarm.

Flames rose faraway. At first, I thought a field had caught fire.

Then a rider galloped by in a panic. He was heading for town. The Dog Heads were attacking.

All of us were frightened. However, Yü became frantic. She started to shout to the driver to go faster.

Unfortunately, our carriage could only lumber along. And that made her even crazier. She began cursing the driver and wouldn't stop even when her mother told her to be quiet.

And when the carriage rolled through a section of road lined with trees, Yü began seeing a Dog Head behind every tree trunk.

I think the trees scared her as much as the threat of the Dog Heads. Yü is a town girl. Her idea of nature is rows of flowers in a garden. Heaven knows what she would make of the Great Forest!

Lin grabbed her and held her while Madame calmed her down.

Ch'ai said that she was glad my guard had come along after all. They might not know drama but they do know war.

I banged on the carriage side for the driver to stop. Then I opened the door and translated the rider's warning for Uncle Muntjac just in case he hadn't understood.

At the Sung estate, Uncle Muntjac had been a fish out of water. But now he was back in his pond. He began barking out orders. Instantly, a warrior darted ahead as the point guard. Two more guards slipped away to either side to watch our flanks. Two more would form the rear guard.

Uncle Muntjac gave me his bow and arrows. At first, I did not want to take them. He said that I had as good an eye as any warrior here, and we might need an extra archer. I have been raised to do my duty no matter what others think. So I reluctantly took them.

Then, taking out his own dagger, he clambered on top of the wagon with the help of the remaining guard.

The driver started to protest but I pointed out to him that the Dog Heads would do worse damage.

Then we set off again. Everyone was silent and tense. It is one thing to watch a silly story-dance about traveling through a wilderness. It is quite another thing to have the wilderness invade.

I wished I had been firmer with Uncle Muntjac. I lay the bow and quiver to the side. Still the Chens looked at me so funny. In their sheltered world, they find it hard to believe in violence — even now.

Lin asked me if I knew how to use the bow.

I said everyone at home had to know how to hunt so everyone practiced archery.

Yü wanted to know if I had ever killed a man.

I snapped that I hadn't, but since they were Master Chen's family, I would see that no harm would ever come to them.

They just kept staring.

I've become a savage princess to them again.

I feel as much of an outsider as when I first came here.

When we got to town, the gates were still open. And the militia was still trying to form up. They will have to learn to respond faster to the Dog Heads or they will be in deep trouble.

No, I can't show this as it is to Master Chen. I'll have to recopy it and refine and shorten it.

Even so, Master Chen will have some interesting reading tomorrow.

Second month, thirteenth day
Morning

The Chen family has changed their attitudes toward me.

With our breakfast, Chi the chef had made onion pancakes like the northern Chinese eat.

Ch'ai ate with her usual dainty nibbles and didn't

peep once. She always dropped her head and studied her pancakes whenever I glanced her way. However, from the corner of my eye, I saw her watching me with horrified eyes when she thought I wasn't looking. She's obviously terrified of me.

Yü, however, is another matter. Now that she's at home, she feels it is safe to torment me again. At one point, she leaned toward me and asked me if she could borrow my sword so she could cut her bread.

I politely said that I didn't have one.

Yü, however, kept on baiting me. She said that she knew I had a sword hidden up my sleeve.

When Yü teases me, I sometimes feel like a clumsy water buffalo being nipped by a quick little dog. I was wary of giving her any more room to make fun of me.

I insisted that I had no sword.

However, all through the rest of breakfast, Yü acted as if she did not believe me. And Ch'ai looked as if she expected me to butcher her sister at any moment. So I rushed through my meal. After asking to be excused, I got up to leave.

As I left, Ch'ai looked relieved, but Yü asked to borrow my sword the next time she had a slice of tough beef.

Then, when I got to the schoolroom, I saw Lin whispering to my fellow students. I thought they would all be afraid of me, too.

However, now that Lin is home, he seems to have gotten past his fear. He was polite, though, when he asked for my essay to copy.

Then he sauntered over to his table. I knew he would replace some of my mud-ware words with golden ones of his own. He calls it improving my work. In the end, his will be so superior to mine that it will seem as if I am the one who copied his.

In the meantime, my schoolmates crowded around. They were convinced that I had taken part in many battles in the Great Forest.

They seem to think that war is like it is in the ancient histories. Fighting seems like such a splendid adventure there. Heroes in chariots roll up and challenge other heroes to single combat. The battles all sound like one splendid sports competition.

They plagued me with questions about weapons and killing.

Finally, I lost my patience. I told them that I was no warrior. The only creatures I had shot were birds. And I had only done that to help feed my family and please my father.

However, they were sure I was lying.

Then I snapped at them that I had never killed anyone. I doubt if I ever could. I am not a savage.

From the doorway, Master Chen agreed. He had

overheard me. I suppose Madame had already described to him the extra entertainment that the Dog Heads had provided last night.

Stepping up on his platform, Master Chen told my schoolmates that I already knew more of Chinese history and literature than most colonists did. That made me more Chinese than they were. However, this was not really about being Chinese but being civilized.

Over the last few centuries, the Chinese themselves hadn't been very civilized. The various pretenders to the imperial throne were little better than barbarians. In their battles with one another, they had also destroyed the great cities and libraries. So many irreplaceable things have already been lost.

That shocked me. I've come to love the books. Destroying them would be like killing my family. So I said I didn't see how anyone could do that.

With a smile, Master Chen said that just proved I was also more civilized than many Chinese. So much had already been destroyed and everyone seemed intent on smashing what little was left. If the Chinese did not stop soon, there would be nothing left. The Chinese, too, would be back to scratching in the dirt for roots.

However, it is in just such places as Kingfisher Hill that civilization might be preserved. And that civilization of the future will be both Hsien and Chinese.

We all stared at Master Chen as if he were crazy. I knew what his servants, his whole family . . . well, what the whole town would think if they heard him now.

So I asked him if he had suddenly gotten a fever.

Master Chen just laughed. I'm to keep writing a history of our homeland. And make sure it's about my people as well as his.

I'm finally beginning to understand why he invited my parents to send a student to him. He's just like my parents. All three of them think several steps ahead into the future.

But was there ever a time when kindness and good-heartedness ruled? It all seems like a childish dream. And yet, isn't Father doing exactly that when he tries to end the feuding?

When I get home, I can't wait to tell him how civilized he is.

I —

It's Mei, Madame's maid. Madame wants to see me.

I suppose she wants to scold the little savage in her house.

That afternoon

Madame was at a table, cutting the stems of flowers and putting them into a vase. She said she finds it calming.

I said we'd all had a more exciting evening than we had expected.

She thanked me for making sure it ended safely.

That caught me by surprise.

Trust Madame to know the etiquette about a Dog Head raid!

I think I stammered something about being happy to do that.

Then she held up the slim scissors she was using on the flowers. And she told me that this was the only sharp weapon a lady should use.

I tried to apologize but she stopped me and went on. She informed me that abnormal times required abnormal actions.

She wants me to give archery lessons to her and to all her children.

I told her that I didn't think either of her daughters would agree to be my pupil. One was too scared and the other too hostile.

Madame is not blind. That is why she was speaking to me in private. Even if she was scared, Ch'ai would obey Madame's wishes, and Madame would see to it personally that Yü would treat me with respect. She was not apologizing for her daughters, but she does think I need to understand them.

I said that I didn't blame Ch'ai exactly. We came from

two different worlds, but I didn't understand what I had done to Yü.

Madame explained that, next to Lin, Yü had always been her grandfather's pet. But then I came along.

I didn't see how I could ever replace her in her grandfather's affection, and I said so.

Madame, however, insists that Yü is jealous of me. She says she's grateful that I have been patient so far with her daughter.

A horrible thought came to me then. I asked her if she was afraid I would hurt Yü.

She admitted that when I first came here she might have entertained that fear. She said there was a phrase for the Hsien. They were "raw" people. On the other hand, the tribes that had been conquered were the "cooked." So she had been expecting a "raw" savage who ate uncooked meat.

I felt surprised — and a little hurt as well. I said that she had gone out of her way to make me feel welcome. There was the room and the clothes — and now the mirror.

Madame replied that it was Master Chen's wish that I should think of the estate as my second home. And so, even though she would have put me into a shed or the stables, she had forced herself to go in the opposite direction.

That made me feel even worse inside. So her kindnesses had only sprung from a sense of duty. But that explained the other half of her behavior — the criticisms and frowns.

Then Madame took my hand and added that she was glad that she had done the right thing.

My words last night had made her realize that. If I depended on them, they would also need to depend on me. I was part of Master Chen's family, too. She had come to think of me as a foundling that had been left at their gate.

When she said that, I didn't care if Yü was trying to hit me with a stick. She's a sister after all.

I couldn't help hugging Madame. That surprised her and she became very stiff. Too late, I realized that I couldn't remember her ever embracing any of her children. Perhaps because she didn't want to muss her hair or clothes.

However, she did put her arms around me and patted me on the back briefly before she pushed me away.

So she will never be like my mother. As she's learned from me, there are many different kinds of people in the world.

After midnight

I am writing this by candlelight because I don't think I'll get back to sleep tonight.

Around midnight, gongs started to sound the alarm.

At first, I thought the Dog Heads were attacking the town itself. So I left my room.

Madame was in the hallway brandishing a hairbrush like a sword. Yü was in the hallway panicking again. Ch'ai was just standing there, dazed and frightened.

I asked Madame what was wrong. She said she didn't know. She obviously wanted to protect her children but didn't know the first thing about it.

I might be hopeless at arranging flowers and my dancing and table manners might be awful, however, this was something I could do. Unfortunately, savage times required a savage princess.

So I shepherded them into Madame's room and told them to stay put. I would find out what was happening.

This time I was the one who was surprised when Madame hugged me. She repeated again that she was glad I was here.

I would have enjoyed the moment if I wasn't feeling just as frightened as they were. Still, I made myself creep down the stairs and then outside into the garden.

Uncle Muntjac had already come over and positioned my guard around the garden. They had drawn their bows ready to repel invaders.

However, they didn't know any more than I did. Uncle tried to hand me a bow but I didn't want to be so conspicuous again. However, I did take his dagger and stuck it in my belt.

It's well I was there. When Lin burst into the garden,

my guard almost shot him. I stopped my warriors just in time. And then I told Lin to go back to his room. I would send word when I found out what was happening.

Then I set out. When my guard fell into step behind me, I told them not to shoot unless I gave the order. After my promise to the Chens, I wasn't about to let the guard kill any of the family and staff — even Chou the gatekeeper.

The servants were even more hopeless than Yü. They were all acting like a flock of chickens being chased by a cat.

So finally, I marched into the outer courtyard and over to the tallest tree. Hiking up my robe around my legs, I hugged my legs to the trunk and pulled myself up to see what I could see.

All I could make out over the rooftops was the palisade. I might have had more confidence if there had been soldiers on the walls instead of frightened townsfolk. They were all peering and pointing in the direction of the mines. And then the news was shouted across the town in frightened, excited voices.

A horde of Dog Heads had attacked the silver mine.

Below me, I heard Uncle Muntjac order someone to stay back. Since he was using the language of the Hsien, I didn't think the other person would understand the warning. And that worried me.

When I looked down, I saw it was Master Chen. He told me calmly to come back inside and to order my escort to get out of sight as well. The townsfolk were scared and might take it out on us.

I thought it was a good idea and shinnied back down. Then Master Chen took us to his study.

The walls are filled with shelves and cabinets full of books. Some of them are truly ancient texts in which the words are written on slips of bamboo and tied together into scrolls. A complete book can be quite heavy and the shelves can even bow under the weight.

The only gap is a small platform where Master Chen sits. Before this platform is a low table on which he has his ink jar in the shape of a tiger's mouth. Next to it is a jade bottle in the shape of a pink gourd. Its water is for mixing his ink. In another jar shaped like a volcano, he has an assortment of brushes, all of different sizes. Master Chen must have been writing even at this late hour because there was a brush with a wet black tip resting on a brush rest in the shape of a mountain range. There was also a miniature screen with inlaid mother-of-pearl carved to look like some gentleman having a picnic. The screen protected the lit candle from drafts.

My guard peered around bored. To them pieces of paper with writing are no better than dirty leaves. And they can't understand why someone would want to fill a whole room with them. To me, it's a hoard of priceless treasure.

Then Master Chen headed over to a tall, dusty cabinet

in the corner. Opening its door, he asked my guard to help him. They took out a suit of antique armor on a stand. The helmet was a close-fitting cap with leather ear pieces that could be tied under the chin. The armor itself was made of small pieces shaped like fish scales that had been sewn together and painted black. Beneath the waist and on the shoulders the small plates were rectangular.

From the depths of the cabinet he pulled out a curious old spear. The spear point has two parts. One is for thrusting. The other is perpendicular to the shaft. That is for cutting or hooking a rider from a horse or a chariot.

Master Chen says that it has been many generations since anyone had used it. He keeps it out of sentiment because his grandfather had purchased it.

However, he guessed he might need it after all. He asked us to help him sharpen the blades. Uncle Muntjac had a small whetstone in his pouch. When he took the spear, he frowned. Then he told me that the wood of the shaft was very brittle. It should be replaced.

What horrible times. Even an elderly scholar has to think about war.

Second month, fourteenth day

It's terrible. The surviving miners have been trickling in all day. The Dog Heads swept in at night. One moment everything was peaceful. The next moment there was a screaming horde killing everyone in sight. And it wasn't just to steal the silver that had been mined. They torched all the buildings. The militia have begun drilling under the watchful eyes of some veterans.

Even though the Dog Heads left, the Sungs have left their estate and come into town. They left so hastily that they didn't have a chance to pack up, so the girls have borrowed clothes, cosmetics, and jewelry from Ch'ai and Yü.

As big as Master Chen's estate is, it's become quite crowded. Everyone has had to double and even triple up in their rooms.

Except for me. No one wants to share a room with the "savage."

The Sungs are just part of a huge group coming into town. The farmers are afraid they'll be next. They've been streaming in from the farmhouses to the safety of the town's walls. All day, water buffalo have been hauling in wagons filled with furniture, clothes, and precious farm tools. They've brought their pigs and chickens as well, so the whole town sounds like a farmyard — and smells like one.

But there is one scent that dominates everything, and that's fear.

Scroll Three

Third Year of the Chung Ta T'ung Era
Second month, sixteenth to thirtieth days

Second month, sixteenth day

Father has summoned me home so there won't be any archery lessons for the Chens.

And because of the Dog Head threat, he's sent two dozen warriors to add to my escort.

It doesn't speak well for the colony's security that they were able to enter the gates unchallenged and wander all through the town. The only problem is that they didn't know where Master Chen's estate was and none of them knew enough Chinese to ask for directions. They tried to use pantomime, but the frightened colonists ran away screaming their heads off. So they wound up wandering back and forth, terrifying most of the town.

It would have been almost comical, but what if they had been a band of Dog Heads?

Fortunately, Uncle Muntjac happened to be getting a drink of water from the well in the courtyard and saw them walking past. He called them in before there was a misunderstanding.

I have to stop now so I can pack —

What's that noise outside my room?

A little later

The Dog Heads have turned the whole world upside down.

I just got back to my room from the strangest meeting.

A servant came to fetch me because the Chinese magistrate himself wanted to meet with me! Amazing. The colonists must really be afraid.

I would have gone right away, but I had to wait until Uncle Muntjac could get his little army in order.

Then we walked toward the large reception hall — or, in my escort's case, swaggered.

The school and household were gathered in the courtyard as we passed. The Sung family watched me pass with new respect.

My little moment of glory was short, though. Madame stopped me to make minute adjustments to my hair and clothes. I was impatient and curious to see what the magistrate wanted, so at first I resented being treated like a small child. But then I remembered how Madame was always doing this even now to Ch'ai and Yü. I guess it meant she now thought of me as one of her family. So I waited, trying to look grateful rather than fidgeting.

When I entered the hall, I found a man in elegant robes seated on a platform in the place of honor. Master Chen was sitting on his left, pouring tea for him.

Master Chen himself introduced me to the magistrate. I barely remembered my manners and bowed in the Chinese fashion.

The magistrate returned my bow and addressed me as "Princess!" I couldn't help hoping that Chou was watching.

The magistrate explained that he had been too busy to call on me before this. He's had two years, so that was a little hard to believe. However, I had seen how my father pretends to accept worse lies from ambassadors. So I just smiled as Father has done. I told him that I was glad he had found the time with all the problems he's had.

Then the magistrate humbly asked me to deliver a letter to my father.

And I —

That was Madame and her children. They had gifts for me so I would remember them. Ch'ai gave me a jade box decorated with birds. Inside is rouge made from flowers.

Lin handed me his treasured tiger belt clasp and told me to hurry back. He would rather copy my homework than do his own.

Then Madame put her hand to her hair and took out the antique kingfisher hairpin. It glittered on her palm as she held it out to me.

I tried to refuse, but she insisted.

Yü became upset. I don't think she realized what her

mother was going to give me. She kept saying that the hairpin was supposed to go to her eventually. I felt bad and I tried to pass it to her. But Madame wouldn't let me. She said she had made no such promise. Yü was going to inherit many other fine things.

Yü was scowling at me fiercely so Lin grabbed her present, which she was holding behind her back.

Lin passed it on to me with the comment that Yü means well.

Her gift is another broad-brimmed straw hat. (And it's soiled from use).

Yü said that when I came back the next time, she hoped that I wouldn't look as dark as a field hand.

I said I hoped there would be a next time.

She laughed and said of course there would. The Dog Heads would take one look at my face and run back to their hills. And then I would go on plaguing and embarrassing her.

I think in her own way, my "sister" Yü will miss me.

I told the Chens I would treasure each item and think of them. And I will. Because each will remind me of my Chinese "family."

Though the rouge is scented, I can also smell animal fat. It won't keep long in this heat. It's not very practical where I'm going, but then Ch'ai has never been very practical herself.

Lin is as sleek and confident as a tiger prowling through the forest so I can look at the belt hook and remember my "other" brother. It's funny that I should have two "tiger-ish" brothers.

And Yü's gift is just typical of her. She can make me angry so many times. And yet, I think I would get terribly bored if she were not around.

Madame's present is like Madame: simple and elegant and refined.

It will be easy to take the smaller items. The hat will mean repacking, though. I wonder if Yü knew . . .

Later

It was Master Chen. He came with two servants, each with a basket. He said that there was no time to write out a homework assignment for me, so he wanted me to read this book and then write what I thought of it.

The first basket was filled with paper.

I was hoping the book in the second basket would be a collection of wonder tales. However, it was a set of silk scrolls. They must have been much loved because the wooden sticks around which the silk was wound were worn from use.

When I unrolled one scroll, I saw that the edges were

ragged and there were moth holes as well as smudge marks from ink-stained fingers.

It was Master Chen's own copy of Master Meng's scrolls.

He explained that he would have given me a better copy, but there was no time. So he was presenting me with his personal set of scrolls.

When I said I couldn't take it, he said he had memorized every word by now.

I promised him I would, too.

I feel so sad at leaving. Why?

Most of the colonists barely tolerate me. The houses, the clothes, the food — everything is still strange sometimes.

It has to be Master Chen.

I wish he and Master Meng were right about kindness and goodheartedness. If there were more people like them in the world I would have more hope.

Second month, seventeenth day
Morning
En route to Kingfisher Hill

We're resting on the way back to Kingfisher Hill.

When we left the colonists' town, Uncle Muntjac insisted that he and the other warriors of the original escort are my honor guard, the princess's own. So they strut in a circle around me with Uncle Muntjac in front. And the rest of the warriors walk in front and in back.

It's strange to pass through the Chinese territory.

It's a lovely spring day. Farmers should be planting the fields. But they're empty. In one field I saw a furrow half-plowed. In front of another house, I saw a bucket with rice seedlings just rotting away. Everywhere, people dropped what they were doing and ran for the town. The land feels so empty now. I almost feel like the ghosts have taken over.

It's odd. Part of me relaxes when it sees the old, familiar sights. However, the other part of me knows Dog Heads could be hiding anywhere. And at those times I feel as if I am stumbling through a nightmare.

And it makes me sad to think of the Sungs' magnificent home standing just as deserted as the farmsteads.

Later that day

We've met the sentries on the edge of the forest. They let out low whistles and imitate monkey calls.

Knowing that they're watching, I feel safer.

I'll change my clothes here. The forest can overgrow the path in days and I don't want to tear my silken clothes on the thorns. But I'll keep the kingfisher hairpin in my hair. I am from Kingfisher Hill after all.

The jujube and litchi trees have flowered while I've been away. The air is filled with a scent sweet as Chinese wine. Perched in a branch, a monkey nibbles at a tiny blossom. We should have a good crop of fruit this autumn.

I'm home. And yet I feel sad to be leaving the Chinese town.

Later that day

We are pushing hard to get home so this break will be short. Uncle Muntjac's old war wound is acting up. I noticed his limp slowing him. It's made him mad, but I ordered this rest even though I'm eager to get home. I won't have Uncle straggling behind us like a stray dog. He lives for his pride.

We're only a li from the town by the edge of the forest. Just beyond the last trees, I can see the first fields. And rising above them is Kingfisher Hill.

The drums are booming. At first, it was like distant thunder but the word spread through the forest. Uncle Muntjac, who knows all the war signals, looks grim. He said the Dog Heads were raiding our lands.

We have to go.

I have to do something or I'll go crazy. So I guess I might
as well write.

By the time we came through the gates, the warriors
had assembled. I could spot the veterans because they
were quiet and grim. The younger warriors were trying to
hide that they were scared by bragging about what they
were going to do to the Dog Heads.

Though they had just had a hard journey from Kao-
liang, my escort immediately peeled away to join the war
band. Uncle Muntjac would have, too, if I had let him. But
that poor old man could never have kept up. I told him I
felt safer with him around. Would he mind staying here?

He hemmed and hawed, but I secretly think he was
glad for the excuse.

I met Father already heading out the door. Besides his
bow and arrow, he was carrying his Chinese war ax. It's
made of iron, not bronze, and is very expensive. He only
took it from its special place on the wall when things were
serious.

I told him I had an important letter, but he said he had
no time for that now.

Little Tiger was there, too, pleading to go. However, Father ordered him not to ask again.

Mother was holding onto Father's arm and looking as

if she were going to cry. And little Begonia was holding onto his leg.

However, when they got to the door, Mother let go and straightened up. She was putting on her official face for the tribe. And she pulled Begonia away, too.

Father made a short speech about doing their best for the tribe. Then the war band moved off in a purposeful group. Those old Chinese veterans back in town would shake their heads because there were no even ranks. And certainly no one marched in step.

However, all Father has to do is signal with his hand and our warriors will melt into the green shadows. They can move as quiet as smoke, and they will fight as bravely as any Chinese soldier.

Once we were back inside the palace, though, Mother began to cry. I've been trying to keep my younger brothers and sisters quiet and not bother her. I've told them some of the Chinese wonder tales until one by one they've fallen asleep.

Second month, eighteenth day
Morning

Father's home. He looks so tired. There were smudge marks on one cheek and a cut on his arm. Many of the warriors also had wounds. Kumquat must have been making salve while I was gone because she pulled out huge jars and began tending to everyone.

As the king, Father was her first victim. Sometimes Kumquat's cures can be worse than the illness. As Father sat wincing, he said the Dog Heads had gotten far worse.

He looked too tired to talk to me about Master Meng's ideas. Instead, I just read him the magistrate's letter.

Incredible!

The magistrate is proposing that we work together against a common enemy.

For a Chinese official to ask for our help . . . well, I guess that tells you how scared they are.

Little Tiger immediately said we can't trust the Chinese any more than we can the Dog Heads.

Father asked me what I thought. I said that if they were all like Master Chen, an alliance would be fine. However, there were too many townsfolk who lumped us together with the Dog Heads.

Father thought about that and then sighed. He has lost many good men. We would need all the help we could get. So he will send out runners and summon the council and get them to approve of talking to the Chinese. I, of course, will act as the interpreter.

I know now that's what my parents had planned all along when they sent me to the Chinese school. I had thought it would be for boring trade and diplomatic matters. I had never expected it to be for something this urgent.

And tomorrow Little Tiger and the other boys from the Ape House will begin training in earnest as warriors.

My mother tried to say they were too young, but Father says in these times children have to grow up fast.

When he said that, he was looking at me rather than Little Tiger.

I won't talk to Father about Master Meng after all. It's a time for swords, not ridiculous dreams.

Second month, twenty-second day

Not much time to write. I hope Master Chen won't be disappointed with me.

The winds have changed. All day they've been blowing from the southeast. They've brought the warm, moist air. Soon the monsoon rains will come.

Even so, the Dog Heads have attacked every night. Francolin and I have been busy caring for the wounded and preparing food for the warriors. Everyone's making arrows and bows or sharpening swords and repairing crossbows.

The young warriors are all veterans now. There's no

laughing or boasting anymore. Just the same silent determination on all their faces when they tramp out of the gates.

And when they come back, there are always some women and children wailing for lost fathers and husbands and brothers.

No one is tending the fields. If this keeps up, we will have a poor harvest. And the men have no time to hunt.

Though it goes against all tradition and honor, I'm beginning to think Father is right. Feuding is no way to live.

We're already dipping into our reserves of food. I will organize the children. Hibiscus and Barbet are old enough to be my deputies. We can hunt the smaller game. There won't be much meat, but they'll make a good broth.

I hate war.

That evening

Between the Dog Heads and the hot, humid air, everyone's in a bad temper. Everyone is waving palm-leaf fans in front of their faces for relief.

I've set the younger children to fanning the wounded with palm leaves. Auntie Goral has even closed down her kiln because of the heat.

As I tend the injured, I find myself missing school more and more.

I think I see a little of what Master Chen was talking about. Civilization isn't just big cities and statues and things. Civilization is being able to walk to school by myself without an armed escort of six warriors.

That much I can understand.

And want.

I wish I'd had time to borrow some other books from Master Chen's library. Instead, I'm stuck with a philosophy book. I've tried and tried to read Master Meng.

However, though my eyes see the words, the thoughts don't come.

Second month, twenty-third day

The weather is miserable. I feel all itchy. I wish I could take off my skin and dump it somewhere.

Everyone's feeling just as irritable. It seems every few moments I must pull one of my siblings off another. Barbet looks at Drongo the wrong way. Begonia doesn't like the clicking noises Hibiscus makes with her tongue. It's a dozen silly things that we would ignore in better weather.

This morning there was a terrible dispute between Francolin and Toad over the silliest thing — Toad had said that Francolin had taken too much water from the storage jar and should replace it. Then Peacock tried to use his authority as steward to silence them. So Francolin and Toad told him they would argue as loudly as they wanted. And the quarrel turned into a three-way fight.

They're still not speaking to one another. Each uses me as a messenger. Before supper, I was kept busy running back and forth between Peacock and Toad over the menu.

I'll try to take my mind off the weather by reading Master Meng again.

A little later

Master Meng is difficult to follow because it's in a series of dialogues, and a lot of the words are beyond my vocabulary.

And yet when I read the words on the silk scroll, I hear Master Chen's voice. The same gentleness. The same hope.

Master Meng said that at heart all humans are good, and that goodness will come out like water pouring down a hill if given the chance.

Master Meng, though, had never met the Dog Heads. Which is why he lived long enough to write a book.

And yet, does it always have to be kill or be killed? Can't we be more than animals eating one another?

And wouldn't it be nice if Father could just be a father and not have to chase Dog Heads every night?

Second month, twenty-fourth day

Dark clouds have been blowing overhead. I can't wait for the rain to fall and bring some relief.

Little Tiger doesn't understand why I have my nose buried in Master Meng's scrolls. If I can't talk with Master Chen, reading Master Meng is the next best thing.

Little Tiger thinks I should be doing something useful like cooking. And my little brothers and sisters want me to play with them or tell them stories. Since they can't read, they can't comprehend that the act of reading, itself, can give pleasure.

Even Francolin thinks it's all right to make noise as she cleans my room.

Only Mother understands.

She tells them to leave me alone.

That evening

As I tend the injured warriors, Master Meng's words seem like a wonder-filled fairy tale.

People must have thought the same thing when he was alive. He wrote that long ago good-heartedness once filled all humans. It was like a forest that covered a mountain. However, every day it was attacked by axes until it disappeared. Now people doubt it ever existed.

Wouldn't it be nice if we could make the world civilized again?

Then every day wouldn't have to be so terrible and sad. I feel like I'm drowning, and the book is the rope that Master Chen has thrown to me.

So even though part of me laughs when I read Master Meng, part of me wants to believe in a sane, peaceful world.

Second month, twenty-fifth day

This is my first chance to write. I have been going in full Chinese robes with my parents to greet the mighty lords and elders of the Hsien who have journeyed here from all over the Great Forest for the council meeting.

My parents greet our honored guests politely and warmly and see that they are settled comfortably into their camps. There are a hundred details such as water and food and whatever else they might require. One lord from the eastern parts wanted a conch shell. Mother, though, did not even blink an eye, but sent Francolin to fetch one from the palace. One group does not want to camp next to another group, so that must be sorted out, too. Mother is good at gently sweeping away their frowns like dust from the veranda.

Our most difficult guest is the lord of Big Rock, Leopard. He objected to everything from his campsite — he tried three different spots — to the way I was clothed. He's such a boor. The other lords were curious, amused, or even charmed. However, he insists that no princess of the Hsien should dress as a Chinese.

Mother and Father almost strained their smile muscles trying to be polite. However, Big Rock also has had its share of kings and have sometimes been our rivals for power. So even if Lord Leopard is rude, he must be treated with respect.

Second month, twenty-sixth day

The council's finally meeting this morning. Through the bamboo walls I can hear them from my bedroom just as Mother must be listening from hers. I know I'm not up to saving civilization. And yet I thought I ought to record an important day like this in my diary. At least I could do that much to satisfy Master Chen.

Great-Uncle Sambar, my grandmother's brother, has been asked to come out of retirement. He's been through many a battle, and has a scar from almost every one of them. Though he only has one eye and limps, his mind is sharp as ever.

When Father told the council about the Chinese proposal, Lord Leopard was all for letting the Chinese stew in their own mess. If the Dog Heads hated the Chinese, the Chinese had only themselves to thank. Besides, the

Chinese had done us no favors. With a little luck, the Dog Heads and the Chinese will destroy each other. A small group of the more foolish support his view.

Others believe that since the Chinese soldiers have marched off, the colonists will be of little help. From what little I've seen of the colonists' militia, I have to agree. However, that's only a small part of the picture. Father's right. If we can learn to trust one another now, we can co-operate even more in the future.

Father pointed out that since the other tribes have refused to stand with us, we need allies where we can get them — even if it is only a few colonists.

In the end, wiser heads side with Father.

It's been decided. We will meet with the Chinese colonists and decide how to deal with the Dog Heads.

Second month, twenty-eighth day

It looks as if it will rain any moment.

Mother tried to get Father to postpone his trip, but he insisted on going.

I stood on the edge of the crowd of servants, shepherding my little brothers and sisters. Father was giving last-minute instructions to Little Tiger who will take his place. My older brother looked scared but proud. However, Mother will really be running things, and Little Tiger is not to make any decisions without asking her.

Then Father spread his arms and called for his little birds. The crowd parted so my little brothers and sisters could run in.

Father swept all four of them off their feet into his strong arms. When he had set them down again, he turned to me.

He smiled and said I was too old to pick up anymore. I was a young woman now and have been through the ceremonies. I agreed — though I would have liked to have been flung into the air, too.

"And you'll help your mother take care of your brother?" he asked.

"Of course," I promised.

He said that he knew things were safe then. He held out his hand and asked if I were too old to take it.

I told him no. With Mother on one side and I on the other, we left the palace and escorted him to the gates.

Hibiscus and Begonia clung to his poncho. They were weeping openly. Drongo and Barbet were doing their best not to cry, but their lips were quivering.

Behind us walked Father's escort, all of them hand-picked warriors. Proud as a general, Uncle Muntjac led them. He had begged me to ask Father to let him go, insisting that Father would need his sword. Since they will be traveling at a regular pace, I figured it would be fine. So I made the request to Father, and he indulged the both of us.

The village gathered all around, cheering.

A warrior began to beat the huge, old bronze drum. The sound boomed down the hill, across the water, and through the forest.

At the gates, Father let go of my fingers. I would have walked with him all the way to the forest. However, he told me that Mother needed me here to keep everyone in line. And so I stayed.

As the villagers cheered from the gates, I watched Father stride off, strong and confident.

I know he will find a way to stop the Dog Heads. With all due respect to my teacher, Master Chen is wrong. It won't be me who will save civilization.

It will be Father.

Second month, thirtieth day

Father is dead.

Uncle Muntjac just stumbled into the village this morning. He was covered with dirt and leaves and sweat, more dead than alive. In his hand, he had Father's ax.

However, he was so out of breath that he couldn't answer any questions. He just limped through the village until he found Little Tiger. Then he knelt and held out the ax to my brother.

He would only have done that if Father were dead.

Everyone began wailing.

I'm too numb to cry, though.

Father can't be dead. He just can't.

Scroll four

Third Year of the Chung Ta T'ung Era
Third month, first to nineteenth days

Third month, first day

When Uncle Muntjac had a chance to rest, he told us about the ambush.

The Dog Heads came out of the forest before our men could draw their bows or raise a sword. Only Uncle Muntjac survived to bring us the news.

I want to kill all the Dog Heads —

I have to stop. My little brothers and sisters have started crying again. Drongo's the worst. I must calm them, even though I'm scared myself.

Later that day

The monsoons have finally come. It's as if heaven was a huge bowl of water that has broken. The rain pours down like a river. It pounds the roofs and makes little streams in the streets. The whole world looks as miserable as I feel.

What's going to happen to us?

No, that's the wrong thing to say.

What would Father do?

We still have most of our warriors, after all. With the help of our allies, we can match the Dog Heads in strength.

Yes, what would Father do?

I'm trying to remember all those times I eavesdropped on his war councils. He would send out replacements for the lookouts. A tired sentry is a dead one.

And word must be sent to the Chinese colonists as well as to the rest of the Hsien.

And Father and his men must be brought back.

I would like to leave Mother more time to mourn. But I'll make these suggestions to her. Then we'll speak to Little Tiger. It will sit better with him if the proposals come from Mother.

Later that day

I should have known that Mother would think of her people before herself.

I found her with old Great-Uncle Sambar, speaking to Little Tiger. He looks as stunned as I feel.

And Great-Uncle Sambar was already advising him to do the things of which I had been thinking. Little Tiger looked dazed but he kept nodding his head.

So I really had no business interfering in my elders' affairs. Great-Uncle Sambar stared at me with his one good eye and asked me what I wanted.

Mother explained that she and Father had often let me listen to their plans. Great-Uncle Sambar said that at times like these I might have to do more than listen. They needed all the good ideas they could get.

I think he was just being polite. At first, I didn't really see what I could do. But they need me to write a letter to the Chinese magistrate.

Great-Uncle Sambar is suspicious of everyone until we can find the traitors. He now insists that the Chinese colonists come to us. They may bring an armed escort, but the guard must wait outside our town and the Chinese leaders themselves must enter unarmed.

He's going to propose that if one of us is attacked, the other will come to his aid. Our palisades have held off the Dog Heads before and should again. And certainly the Chinese town's huge palisades will keep out the Dog Heads even better than ours.

I just hope he can read my handwriting.

Third month, second day
Afternoon

The roosters are so drenched that they can only manage short pathetic crows.

It was the signal, though, for Great-Uncle Sambar to

lead the war band through the gates. Despite the down-pour, they brought back Father and his men.

The Dog Heads have taken their heads.

I go crazy when I think of Father's head rotting in some Dog Head cave.

The Dog Heads are savages who should be crushed like so many maggots. I hate Dog Heads. I don't care what Master Meng says. I want them all dead. Then I'm going to do to them what they did to Father.

That evening

Over the roaring rain, I have heard axes and hammers and chisels all day. There are so many coffins to make.

I try to calm the little ones by reciting the Chinese stories that I've read, but my voice is getting hoarse.

And they're too busy crying to listen.

Third month, third day

Though it was raining, we buried Father.

The Chinese have priests who specialize in finding lucky grave sites. However, our priests do it differently.

First, they sacrificed the best of our water buffalo. Then the wooden coffins were carried on poles with the whole village following behind them. In front of them was a priest who threw eggs, one by one.

Sometimes the water fell like a silvery curtain so it was hard to breathe — let alone see the priest. All each of us could do was follow the person ahead of him or her.

Despite our straw raincoats, we are as soggy as fish. I had to keep a special eye on Drongo and Hibiscus because they're so young.

The priest must have gone through a whole basket of eggs but they kept breaking. Finally we reached the grassy spot on the riverbank where my family had had our last picnic. That seems an eternity ago.

Here the egg landed and just rolled to a stop. It was a sign from Father that he wanted to be with his kingfishers.

The river is much higher and broader now from all the rain and runoff. Despite the rain, I glanced down the riverbank. The kingfisher burrows had been dug high enough to be safe.

Little Tiger ordered the men with the shovels to dig the graves. And we buried Father and his warriors there.

But there is still no time to cry.

Third month, sixth day

I'm exhausted. I don't see how Mother and Little Tiger do it. Even though it has been pouring steadily, lords have been coming from all over the Great Forest. Peacock, Francolin, and the other servants are exhausted trying to make so many unexpected visitors comfortable.

The Hsien everywhere are in a panic. They have to be reassured. Orders have to be given for the defense.

Fortunately, there are no banquets to be planned. Because we are in mourning, all our food is uncooked so meals are simple.

I have been helping my brother and mother in whatever small ways I can. I receive each new group at the gates. Often I have to play the peacemaker as well. I have seen Mother do it before so I can do that much. However, it is all acting. Inside, I want to wail like my little brothers and sisters.

I try to help Kumquat with my brothers and sisters. She's really getting too old for this sort of thing. They have to be fed, kept clean, and dressed. And they always want to keep Mother in sight now that they've lost Father. Yet they can't be allowed to make noise, which is hard because there always seems to be one of them whimpering and ready to cry.

Maybe I can distract them with Mustafa's shells. I hope Mustafa is well. When last I saw him, he was planning to leave. I hope he did before the Dog Heads' attack.

The shells did the trick for a while.

Then Barbet put them down. He asked me if we were going to die, too. And then the others started worrying, too.

I've promised them that they'll be safe. They're so trusting. They believe me. I don't know why.

That evening

Ugh. The delegation from Big Rock just arrived. I was hoping the constant rain would keep them away. Lord Leopard bulled through the gates, insisting that Little Tiger is too young and that he should lead the Hsien.

I couldn't stop him. He stormed into the palace. I can hear him now trying to browbeat my older brother.

Lord Leopard claims Father's death is an elaborate Chinese plot. He says it is the Chinese colonists who betrayed Father. The Chinese are trying to get us to do all the fighting. He says the Chinese want us to attack the Dog Heads by ourselves. They would love to see the tribes battling one another while they sit like vultures on the side waiting to kill the weakened winner.

Lord Leopard wants all the Hsien to attack the Chinese colony now.

That's just outrageous!

Little Tiger is insisting that he is the king. Sometimes it's good that he's stubborn.

But he's considering Lord Leopard's plan to attack the Chinese.

I will have to talk to Little Tiger as soon as Lord Leopard leaves.

Later that evening

I didn't have to charge in on Little Tiger. He called for me. Mother and Great-Uncle Sambar were there, too.

They wanted to know if I thought Lord Leopard was right. I said I thought the Chinese were sincere. They wouldn't attack their strongest ally.

Great-Uncle Sambar says that when he was a boy, he can remember when the war band had to battle Chinese slavers and squatters. And there is a long list of tribes that no longer exist because of the Chinese.

I did my best for Master Chen's people. I said that when Great-Uncle Sambar was a boy, the Chinese colonists would never have let a Hsien girl go to one of their schools. But times have changed. And that's been proven by my own experiences. Besides, the Chinese colonists are just as frightened of the Dog Heads as we are.

Mother agrees with me, but Great-Uncle Sambar still

isn't convinced. At least, Little Tiger is wavering rather than believing Lord Leopard.

But that raises another question that's even more disturbing. If it wasn't the Chinese colonists, then it has to be someone on the council who betrayed Father.

But who?

Third month, ninth day

The monsoons have stopped temporarily. It's a relief to dry out everything.

While it was raining, however, the Dog Heads stayed away. Will the raids start again?

At least Little Tiger is going to carry out Father's plan.

So perhaps my parents were right. It was good to send me to a Chinese school. Or we'd be at war with them right now.

This time, though, the Chinese colonists must come to us. And only one of them will be allowed inside. The rest must wait outside the walls.

I —

The alarm drums are booming. Oh, no! The Dog Heads are attacking!

We're not ready.

It was a false alarm.

It was only the colonial militia escorting the magistrate. They're going to camp for the night and will arrive tomorrow. The drummer misunderstood the message from the sentries.

Of course, when I went out onto the veranda, I didn't know that yet. I'm just grateful it wasn't the Dog Heads.

The whole capital had panicked. Frightened children and elders jammed the streets, trying to escape. Unfortunately, they blocked the warriors who were trying to get to the palisade.

They hadn't even closed the gates!

Almost everybody had a good laugh when the confusion was sorted out. Only Great-Uncle Sambar and Mother and myself weren't smiling. It's no joke.

What if it had really been the Dog Heads?

Poor Francolin is still shaking. I'd better calm her.

Third month, tenth day
Morning

As the official interpreter, I was at the gates with Little Tiger and Great-Uncle Sambar. Everyone else was on the palisade, watching as the Chinese came. Chinese traders have passed through the area, but this was the first time so many had arrived. And the Hsien people were as curious about the Chinese as the Chinese were about them. As the militia stumbled through the mud, I could see the colonists craning their necks to catch a glimpse of us. The magistrate wasn't in his carriage this time. Instead he was mounted on a magnificent charger. He was in polished armor made of iron scales.

When I first saw the militia, I didn't know whether to laugh or cry. I had never seen such an outlandish bunch. Their armor ranged from coats of cloth to expensive shirts of lacquered plate that clacked as they walked. One soldier was in an armor made out of rhinoceros hide!

And they had all sorts of weapons. Some of them were kitchen cleavers tied to bamboo poles. Others had swords too ornate to be anything but home decorations. The mechanisms of some of the crossbows looked more like rust than metal.

There were some old veterans acting as officers and sergeants. They're better armed and armored. I could hear them trying to shape the amateur warriors into a military column, but it was hopeless. It was like watching dogs chasing hens.

However, one suit of armor looked awfully familiar. Suddenly, the man in it waved and I heard Master Chen call to me. I realized it was the antique armor from his study. It was strange to see it suddenly have legs.

So even my elderly teacher has been drafted.

Next to him was a militiaman in a leather vest who also waved. When he took off his fancy plumed helmet, I saw it was Lin.

Suddenly, I felt sick. I thought again of what Chou had said and was ashamed. I really didn't want my master and schoolmate to see our capital and our "palace" where the animals slept. One look and they would both be making jokes like Yü.

Both Master Chen and Lin tried to step out of line to greet me, but a huge old warrior shouted them back into formation.

I was glad Mother had insisted that I wear my Chinese clothes and shoes, but I was still nervous. I stumbled a bit over the words when I began interpreting.

After the official greetings, Great-Uncle Sambar made it clear that he still does not trust the Chinese. Only the magistrate was to be allowed inside. The magistrate wanted his clerk to record the meeting. Great-Uncle Sambar, though, didn't want a young, strong colonist inside the walls.

Both Great-Uncle Sambar and the magistrate were equally stubborn. I was afraid the meeting might have ended there. I could see Master Chen pointing at himself eagerly. I still was afraid of what he would say when he saw how I lived. And yet it was better to be personally embarrassed than to have the talks break down, so I suggested Master Chen as an alternative.

Great-Uncle Sambar squinted his one good eye at Master Chen and must have decided that an elderly, stoop-shouldered scholar was no danger to the capital.

Master Chen took a basket from Lin's back and walked through the mud. He seemed as happy to see me as I was to see him. But he had brought me a basket of homework.

As I sighed and took it, I asked him what Master Meng would make of him in his warrior outfit. He said he was fighting to end fighting.

I was glad I was able to quote Master Meng back to him. I told him that if we do not believe in compassion, a kingdom will be hollow.

It cheered him to hear that I had been doing my assignment after all.

As we proceeded to the palace, he brought me quickly up to date on the rest of his family. Madame and Ch'ai were making quilted vests for militiamen to wear beneath their armor. Master Chen was wearing their handiwork underneath his. I could see Madame's tiny, even stitches. The entire colony is getting ready for war.

Both family members and servants are taking archery

lessons from an old sergeant. Yü has challenged me to a competition when I get back.

At the same time that he talked, he was glancing around. I kept waiting for him to smirk. However, even though Master Chen's dressed like a warrior, he's still a curious scholar at heart. He was fascinated by everything and asked countless questions.

When he came to the palace, he went over and felt the posts that held it up. He would have stayed outside studying the construction, but the magistrate impatiently called him inside.

I don't know why I was worried about Master Chen. He's not like his gatekeeper, Chou. Master Chen is a civilized man. Civilization isn't about fancy clothes and shoes and mansions. It's about having an open mind. Despite the differences, the Hsien are his equals. Too bad there aren't more people in the world as civilized as him.

The only bad moment came when we climbed up the ladder to the veranda. Kumquat was standing there scowling at the Chinese just as Chou had frowned at me. Then she started making signs to ward off evil.

When Master Chen asked me what she was doing, I made the mistake of lying and saying that she was greeting him. He was so mortified because he thought the Chinese must have offended Little Tiger. He almost copied Kumquat's gestures. However, I stopped him by lying again and saying that it was only appropriate for women to greet someone that way.

The discussion itself was long and difficult. The Chinese magistrate wants to be cautious. He plans to fight a defensive war. Let the Dog Heads wear themselves out assaulting the palisades first.

I guess that's the Chinese way of thinking. Far to the north, the Chinese built a Great Wall to keep out the barbarian hordes. It didn't work up there, and I don't think it will work down here, either.

In the end, he offered no help for our war band. However, he did agree to come to our aid if we were attacked. And we will do likewise.

It's not what we had hoped for. It's difficult to beat the Chinese on a deal.

It was late afternoon by then, so we all started to eat.

Though it isn't raining, the ground is quite muddy and slippery. I suggested sending food and drink to the Chinese militia outside the palisade. Of course, Great-Uncle Sambar got up all upset. He was against dipping into our stores, saying that they could eat their own rations. I asked Mother if we shouldn't show the colonists what hospitality really was, and in the end, we included the rest of Master Chen's militia-mates in the meal.

As we ate, I remembered that Master Chen had a little shrine to the dead in his house. I think it's a good idea. It would be easier to talk to Father. I asked my teacher if he thought it would be all right if I did it, too.

Master Chen had met my father. He said he thought Father was close to me, shrine or no shrine. But it couldn't hurt.

After our meal, as we escorted the magistrate and Master Chen back outside, I told my teacher I was still reading Master Meng. And he laughed and said he was busy reading a manual on warfare that he had found in his library. He hadn't even known that he'd had it. He showed it to me. Every spare moment, he reads aloud to the others. They're all like his students back at school.

Master Chen is a clever man. Even so, I don't think he can learn enough. And the final test will not be failure but death.

At least he has lived a full life. What about Lin, though?

I feel sorry for him and yet I'm also afraid of him. He won't be as understanding as his grandfather. I know he will tease me mercilessly. However, I can't put it off anymore.

Third month, eleventh day
Morning

I helped bring breakfast out to the militia this morning. I could tell the farmers and hunters. They look a little stiff from sleeping on the damp ground. However, the towns-folk are miserable.

Lin sat with his arms wrapped around himself shivering. I'm sure he missed the comforts of his own room. Making fun of my home is the last thing on his mind right now.

I told him hot rice porridge was just the thing to warm his insides.

Right away he forced himself to sit up and grin in his old confident way. I don't think he wants me feeling sorry for him. As he ate, we finally had a chance to chat. I wanted to find out more about our schoolmates and about my "adopted" family. (As their teacher and grandfather, everyone would have kept Master Chen from knowing the really delicious gossip.)

However, Lin merely said that they were all fine. Usually, I can't get him to stop talking, but he seemed more interested in his meal. So I asked him how he was getting along with the Sungs. The boys were just as conceited as Lin so I expected there would be disagreements. And I thought Madame and the Sungs would have more opportunities to try to make a match between Lin and one of the Sung girls.

However, all Lin said was that the Sungs were also fine.

I thought it was his journey through the Great Forest that had so subdued him. It was one thing to talk boldly about it at the Sung estate and quite another thing to walk through it. Or perhaps this dreadful march hadn't matched his schoolboy fantasies about war.

So I asked him if he needed anything else. He set down his bowl and stared at me hard. Then he asked if I thought his family would survive the war.

I said, How should I know?

He thinks that because I can shoot a bow I'm a warrior. He's not at all like the blustery schoolmate I've always known. It's the first time he's ever admitted that I might know something that he doesn't. I wish I could oblige him with an answer, but I'm as frightened as he is.

In normal times, back at school, he is king of the roost. Right now, though, he's like a bird tied up and bound for the chopping block.

I tried to tell him to have faith in the colony's defenses. But he got mad and said not to patronize him. So, I finally had to confess that I didn't know.

He considered that for a moment and then gave me his old smile. He told me that all the colonists said the Hsien have a lot of magic. They ought to be able to read the future. I said, Send those Hsien to me. I would love to know what was going to happen. We both had a good laugh at ourselves.

I never suspected we had the same sense of humor. (A scary idea!) I look forward to getting to know him better — if school ever reopens again. No, I have to follow my own advice and have faith myself.

I *will* see him again.

That afternoon

Master Chen and Lin have left. They waved a cheerful farewell as they marched away. I tried to smile and wave back. But I wonder when I will return to school. Will I even see my teacher again? Or my Chinese family?

In the meantime, I have a basket of homework waiting for me. But first, I will write Father's name on a tablet of wood. Then I'll gather the other things for the shrine. I don't have incense sticks, but I'll get some sweet-smelling herbs from Toad. And I'll collect some tidbits, as well, to send his ghost to eat. And maybe Francolin can get some cool, sweet coconut milk to drink, too.

That evening

I asked Great-Uncle Sambar to make Mother and Little Tiger rest. And he agreed. They're trying to do too much. Despite all the work, they listened to his suggestions and rested for an evening. So our family can be alone at last.

When I showed them the shrine and explained what it was, my little brothers and sisters began to cry. So did Little Tiger. So did Mother. She doesn't have to be brave in private. Neither do I.

I will never again see Father smile.

And so I'll never feel warm and safe again.

Have to stop. My tears might smudge the page. And that will never do in an official history.

Third month, fifteenth day
Evening

The drum is booming out to signal the assembly. Drums in the other neighboring villages are echoing, carrying the message across the entire Great Forest.

A scout has sent word. The colonists are under attack. And this is no false news. We can all see the column of smoke dimming the moon. It's from the direction of the colonists' town.

Our warriors are already running to the muster point. Great-Uncle Sambar will lead the bulk of the war band to help our Chinese allies.

Little Tiger will stay behind with the younger warriors and some veterans. He will wait until enough warriors come from the other villages and follow after Great-Uncle Sambar.

Poor Francolin has fallen to pieces again. I should calm her. However, I can't help thinking of Master Chen in his funny antique armor. How can he fight off the Dog Heads when Father couldn't? And what of my promise to Madame to protect my Chinese family? I can't just sit at home like last time. I have to do something even if I will be the only girl in the war band.

Francolin is too upset to notice me leave.

I can't wear my poncho, though. Everyone would recognize its fancy embroidery. So I'll get an old one of Little Tiger's. I've also got my Chinese straw hat from Yü. That should cover my face. If I stay at the tail of the war band, no one should notice me at night.

I will take the diary and writing tools so I can record tonight. I can tuck them in my quiver. If I don't, I know Master Chen will scold me. And even though the times are so crazy, writing reminds of better, more peaceful times.

Third month, sixteenth day
Morning
Kao-liang

I am writing these words in the ruins of the town while I wait to leave.

At first it gave me some satisfaction that Little Tiger was telling anyone and everyone that he was disappointed about not leading the war band. He was staying and I was going.

I had a scare, though, as we went through the gates. In all the commotion, no one noticed me join the end of the group with my hunting bow and quiver of arrows. However, Mother herself was by the gates to see us off. I pulled my hat down low and tried to strut like a rooster. No one said anything, but I didn't dare stop my rooster-walk until we were out of sight of the village.

It was a hard journey through the Great Forest. Though we had torches, men still tripped over rocks and roots.

Though Uncle Muntjac had gone along as a guide, the pace took its toll. Nine li from town, he began to limp along. Poor old warrior. He tried his best, but eventually he wound up at the rear where I was.

I wasn't sure what to do. He looked so determined to keep up, but he was wincing in such obvious pain.

Finally, I said in a gruff voice that I would help him. However, when I tried to put his arm over my shoulders, he saw my face as I knew he would.

I told him not to say anything and I'd get both of us there. The war band needed a reliable guide with two good legs. But he shook his head and he shouted to Great-Uncle Sambar. When Great-Uncle Sambar saw me, he said he didn't know whether to be angry at me or scared of what my mother would do to the both of us when we got home. Though he was glad enough to have a guide who could act as an interpreter, he still had his doubts. He had seen how well I used a bow when I hunted. It was one thing to shoot a wild partridge. But could I kill a fellow human?

A month ago, I don't know if I could have. After Father's death, though, I knew I could. And I said so.

He commanded me in no uncertain terms to return to the rear of the band as soon as we encountered the Dog Heads.

We made Uncle Muntjac as comfortable as we could and left him singing a bawdy song that I cannot put into a refined book like my history. As we snaked through the forest, lookouts in the trees hooted down to us. It was an oddly comforting sound.

However, when we reached the border of the colonists' territory, we could barely see the moon now because of all the smoke rising. Great-Uncle Sambar ordered our skirmishers to warn us of ambushes. So we double-timed it along the road past the silent farmsteads and empty fields. All around us ran the skirmishers.

As we got closer, I could see how the belly of the column of smoke glowed a fiery red.

However, when we got to the town, it was already too late. The mighty palisade that everyone had expected to protect Kao-liang for weeks or months had already been breached in several places. The giant logs were tumbled about like twigs.

How could this have happened?

Through the gaps we could see the buildings were burning. All sorts of things were scattered in the street. Cabinets, a stool, robes, a lady's vanity chest. I guess looters had taken them from the houses and then dropped them when they found something better. Clothing lay tossed all over.

Then I realized there were people inside the robes. The townsfolk had been massacred. Some of them were covered in arrows. The smell of blood made me sick. Some of the other Hsien were sick, too.

The air stank of the fiery brandy and wine that the colonists make. That had been one bit of loot the Dog Heads valued.

Great-Uncle Sambar told us to keep a sharp lookout. Then he knelt to examine the arrows. Every tribe makes its arrows differently. These had the markings of the Dog Heads.

Jumping to his feet, he began to examine the ground around the wall breaches. The dirt was covered with lots of tracks. However, Great-Uncle Sambar squinted one eye. He pointed to a huge circular depression and said that was made by an elephant.

I felt a cold hand grip my heart. There were wild elephants in the forest, but I had only heard stories about tame ones that the great kingdoms to the south used in war. It takes a great deal of food to feed war elephants, as well as good organization. I would never have expected it of the savage Dog Heads, and I said so.

Great-Uncle Sambar said that we had all made a mistake in underestimating them. For the colonists' town, it had been a fatal error.

I guess it doesn't matter how the Dog Heads did it. They have elephants and we have to deal with them, too.

I felt so unclean surrounded by so much death. I don't know if I can ever wash away this feeling.

Great-Uncle Sambar called for us to enter the town. I must find out what's happened to the Chens.

Later

I'm writing this during a break before we leave the colonists' town. No time for elegant words. I mustn't forget what I've seen.

I owe Master Chen that much.

We found my teacher in the ruins of the marketplace.

He had made his stand before a group of children. His antique armor had not protected him. There were huge gaping wounds in his chest. And the ancient spear shaft had shattered the first time he had tried to use it. It was just as Uncle Muntjac had warned. I guess he hadn't had the time to replace it. Though he was weak, he told us that the elephants had been guided by Chams from the south who had tied swords to the tusks. Arrows and spears had just glanced off their tough hides. Once the wall had been broken in several places, the Dog Heads had poured through and made short work of the inexperienced defenders. As a sign of contempt, the colonists had been left their heads.

Some of the colonists had been taken away as slaves, though. He begged Great-Uncle Sambar to help any of the Chen family who were alive. Great-Uncle Sambar said he would do what he could. However, we both knew it wouldn't be much.

Master Chen's breathing became ragged. I took off my poncho and made a pillow for his head. He had always been so kind to me. Then I took off my hat and asked him what else I could do. I thought he might like some water, and I could fetch it in that. However, to his last breath, Master Chen was still the teacher. He pleaded with me. "You will want revenge. But the dead are not important. It's the living that count." And then with a sigh, he died.

Great-Uncle Sambar gave me his own poncho to wear. And when I had translated my teacher's last words, Great-Uncle Sambar shook his head. "If someone takes your hen," he said, "you take one of his. And if someone kills your cousin, you kill one of his family. It only makes common sense."

Is Great-Uncle Sambar right? Is feuding part of our very natures?

Or is Master Chen right? Are we capable of more than killing?

I wanted to cry, but by now there were so many dead that I had cried myself dry. I just knelt there sobbing but no tears would come.

After a few moments, Great-Uncle Sambar said we had to move on. We had to find the surviving colonists and then head back to Kingfisher Hill. There was no telling if that was the Dog Heads' next objective.

When I asked him to let me bury my teacher, he said there was no time.

That nearly made me cry again, but Master Chen himself counted his body as less important than his family.

I begged Great-Uncle Sambar to give me some men so I could go to look for the Chens. However, he refused, saying he had only promised to do what he could. It was too risky to stay long.

I'm afraid I became shameless. I threatened to tell Mother that it was his idea for me to accompany the war band. If there was one thing Great-Uncle Sambar feared worse than the Dog Heads, it was Mother. And in that fear he was a wise man.

So grumbling, he detailed a squad to go with me. But we were only to go to the Chens' estate and back.

I led them on a run to Master Chen's home. The gates

hung half off their hinges and flames were rising from the buildings.

My squad wanted to go back, but I said I was going on. And if I didn't come back, they could explain to my mother that they had left me on my own. That shamed them.

Bodies lay everywhere. Wu the steward, Mei the maid, Chi the chef. Each had been hacked brutally.

However, when I didn't see Master Chen's family, I went into the inner courtyard and buildings. The Dog Heads had destroyed the lovely little garden as well. They had trampled the flowers and hacked down the ornamental trees.

I found Master Chen's cousins, but there was no sign of Madame and her children. So perhaps they have escaped.

Next to his family, Master Chen loved his books best. So I doubled back to Master Chen's study.

The Dog Heads had been here, too, tearing up many of the paper and silk scrolls. And the bamboo and wooden scrolls had been smashed and chopped. This was worse than the massacre of the town. This was the destruction of ages of thought and wisdom.

And for a moment, I lost hope. I felt as if the sun would never rise. There would only be the endless dark night.

Then we heard a groan in a corner. It was Chou, the gatekeeper, who had given me such ugly looks before. A pile of torn-up scrolls had been set on fire. Though he was badly cut up, Chou had dragged himself back and forth to a well to get buckets of water to put out the flames. I could see his blood striping the floor.

He told me I was so lucky to be able to read. He'd always envied me.

I guess that's why he had always acted so meanly.

I was going to try to help him. He said not to bother. It was the library that was important.

He died a moment later.

By then, my men were shouting that the fire was spreading to the study from another building. I felt like I was losing my father and Master Chen all over again.

There wasn't much time. And that gave me another problem. When you have so little time, what do you save from the wisdom of the ages?

I shouted at the squad to fetch baskets. Then I started to pull the scrolls of my favorite books of fables and legends. However, I could feel Master Chen's ghost frowning at me. So I took some of his beloved philosophy books. And then I realized that wasn't enough, either. Though I didn't know the titles, I raced along the shelves snatching the scrolls of history books, too. And some art. And some poetry and geography. There was no time to pick out what was best.

Maybe that's as it should be. My taste in books might

not be the same as another person's. What I rescued might not be what another person would save. And so a random selection might reflect a wider range of tastes.

As I filled a basket, I had one of the squad take it out and bring me another. The other warriors I set to keeping the flames back as long as they could.

Finally, they shouted to me that the fire had spread to the roof. It would cave in at any moment. In blind desperation, I grabbed a shelf-load of scrolls and stumbled out of the study. There were flames and smoke everywhere.

I almost dropped the books when an ember burned my arm. Determined, I hugged the books to me. Coughing, I stumbled out of the house. I just stood there panting in the fresh air. The others beat the flames from my sleeve.

Oh, no. I've just looked at some of the titles for which I had risked our lives. Some of them are scrolls of grammar!

Well, I guess a book is a book.

Somehow, though, I don't think the children of the future will thank me for saving *those* particular volumes.

Third month, seventeenth day
Morning
En route to Kingfisher Hill

We are taking a short rest a few li from the colonists' town.

On the way back home, we picked up some of the

surviving colonists. However, many of them fled from us. They thought we were Dog Heads.

One of them was a woman who was stumbling through the fields. There was something familiar, though, about her back. I told two warriors to bring her to me. When she heard them coming after her, she tried to run but fell. She kept crawling on her hands and knees through the dirt. She screamed when they caught her and she kicked and clawed. I told them to be gentle with her and they were — even though she made it difficult.

Her hair was dirty and tangled with mud and leaves. Her robe was torn and covered with patches of soot. And one foot was without a shoe. And terror had twisted her elegant face into a mask of fear.

But I still recognized Madame.

She calmed down when I put my arms around her and told her my name. However, when I asked her where her children were, she could only shake her head sadly.

So I asked her one by one. "Lin?"

She screwed up her face as she tried to think. Finally she admitted that she did not know where he was. She had also lost track of Yü.

Then I asked her about Ch'ai.

She barely croaked out, "Dead."

And she began to weep. I could only guess when and how her older daughter had died.

What horrible memories.

And I wept, too, because I had failed to protect my Chinese family.

Madame won't talk now. I have cleaned her face and borrowed a poncho for her. She just walks along in a daze. She will eat and drink if something is put into her hands. But otherwise she must be led.

She's simply a shell of the woman I knew. Every time I look at that poor creature, I want to cry again.

Later

We are within sight of the Great Forest.

The lookouts spread the word from the treetops with hoots and whistles. So the village will not be surprised when we finally arrive at the gates.

Late afternoon

We've picked up Uncle Muntjac. He is none the worse for wear except for a few mosquito bites.

Madame and the other refugees are terrified of the Great Forest. They seem to think there's a tiger or monster lurking behind every tree. It's all we can do to keep them from bolting. What do they think of us who are at home in the forest? I suppose we're almost as monstrous.

When he saw Little Tiger and Mother waiting at the gates, Great-Uncle Sambar told me to go ahead first.

I told him that I never expected him to act like a coward.

He shrugged and said I was mistaking prudence for cowardice.

Mother was furious at first, but then she saw the burn marks on my clothing and the blood. I told her that the blood was from Master Chen. I felt like crying all over again.

Mother hugged me hard. "I'm glad you're home, but you had me worried sick." Then she let me go. "But we're not finished yet."

And then she had to become the queen again and not my mother. She grew pale when we told her about the elephants. Little Tiger looked frightened. Well, I guess we all are.

I can hear her and Little Tiger in the next room. They're sending swift runners to warn the other villages about the even greater threat.

I have to stop now. Kumquat wants to clean me up.

And from the stink in the air, she's brewed one of her healthy tonics. I suppose that's my punishment for going.

Mother has ordered a separate house for Madame. Mother says it is the least she can do for my second "mother."

Peacock and our other servants are busy with the other Chinese refugees, so I've sent Francolin to take care of her.

I have tried to make Madame as comfortable as I can. Francolin has already helped clean her up. Francolin doesn't seem so nervous now. She really pities Madame and fusses over her constantly. Meeting someone with worse woes has taken Francolin's mind off her own worries.

I brought Madame the Chinese clothes so she could look more like the Madame I know. However, she sat there like a wooden statue. I had to dress her. I'm afraid the sleeves and hem that were altered for me are a bit short on her.

I was pleased to see that Francolin had already combed her hair. However, Madame would never let it hang down like that. So Francolin and I put her hair up in loops. I feel so clumsy though. Yü would be angry at what we have done to her mother's once-elegant hair.

I had also brought the gifts Madame had given me. I held up the antique mirror. I hoped she would recognize it. Maybe it would help her find her senses. However, she just stared at it and her reflection blankly.

Nor did she remember the hairpin. I set it in her hair, anyway. It was a cheerful blue patch in the black nest of hair.

Perhaps she will remember some day. But is that really kind? It will mean she will also recall that terrible night.

That evening

Little Tiger has sent messengers to the rest of the Hsien that the war band is not assembling after all, but that the lords should come for a council meeting.

As king, Little Tiger has moved out of the Youth House and into my parents' bedroom.

Though Mother has her own room, she's asked to sleep with me. I think she's lonely.

And my little brothers and sisters are so scared they want to be with her as well. So we're all crowded together in my bedroom.

They're all trying to snuggle close to her. Drongo and Hibiscus might start out next to her. However, Barbet and Begonia keep worming their way in so that Drongo and Hibiscus wind up on the outside. It's like watching piglets squirming.

As comical as the sight is, it makes me feel safer in a way and yet also sad.

It's one more sign of change.

Third month, eighteenth day
Morning

I feel guilty. So many of the books are just random choices pulled from the shelves. If only there hadn't been a fire. If only Master Chen had been able to tell me what to save.

I can't even say I did my best. Sometimes I grabbed what was nearest my hand. Even so, I would love to sit down and just browse through my harvest, but there isn't any time.

My little brothers and sisters want to know if I've got any more stories. Drongo is demanding to know if there are any dragon tales. I won't know what I have until I make an inventory. Some of the titles, though, look like they're in archaic Chinese so I'll just have to do my best.

That afternoon

One of the books is about animals. Maybe there's something on elephants. I'll keep that one out!

Later

Ha! I've caught Kumquat. I know her secret.

I decided to store the books so I went to the sheds where we always keep the trade goods. They ought to have been empty.

But when I took the first basket of books into one, I was surprised to find it already full of jars and baskets. Though the walls still smelled of cinnamon, I was even more surprised to hear all the hissing and croaking.

I was going to lift a lid but Kumquat suddenly popped up behind me and slapped my hand away. She told me not to touch it if I valued my life. She acted as if I were a toddler who had tried to touch a bowl of boiling water.

Of course, I was curious and demanded to know what was in it. She was very shifty for a while. I knew better than to threaten to tell Mother on her. Kumquat knew secrets about me that I didn't think Mother needed to hear. However, Kumquat could never say no to me, which had made her a wonderful friend but a terrible guardian. I often got caught up in some mischief. If she had not once been my mother's nursemaid as well, she would have been sent away long ago.

So I wheedled and I coaxed. I knew how to bend her like a green reed.

Finally, she made me swear not to tell Mother. When I promised, she poked her head out to make sure that no one could overhear. Then she whispered to me that she was making the old magic.

I had heard of the old magic from the campfire stories. With the old magic you could create magical servants who could kill rich enemies and then steal their treasure.

I didn't believe in it, however, I had thought of them as tales to frighten children.

My people had practiced it before the Chinese had come, and some tribes in the remote areas still did. I realized I didn't have the first idea of how one went about creating the old magic. The storytellers had been vague about those details. I figured that maybe that had been deliberate.

I was both fascinated and horrified. "What's in there?" I asked. "It sounds alive."

Proudly Kumquat lifted a lid like a cook showing off her favorite recipe. "It's one of the Five Clans." However, inside the basket were dozens of frogs. From their bright colors I recognized that they were poisonous.

Baskets in another corner had scorpions. A third had small but deadly, wriggling snakes. A fourth held millipedes. A fifth had lizards. Each group was in a separate part of the shed.

Suddenly, I felt like there were ants crawling underneath my skin. Forget magic. There was enough venom in that one shed to kill a village.

When I asked her how she had gathered all these animals, Kumquat winked at me. She had enlisted the help of all the elderly grannies and aunties in all the villages to gather as many of the five families of noxious creatures as they could find. "Young people like your mother and you don't put any faith in it anymore. But some of my generation still remember the old magic," Kumquat had said.

I could just imagine all the old women from our capital limping about the jungle gathering all those deadly creatures. "But how do you feed them in the meantime?"

Kumquat told me she used sweets from the pantry to bribe the children to get bugs and other small creatures to feed the Five Clans.

And then I remembered something else she had said. "Villages?"

Kumquat had spread the word among all the elderly Hsien. So in the heart of every village was a collection just like this.

When I asked her what she was going to do with them, she made me promise solemnly to use the secret only for the good of our people. For if the old magic was misused, it could take a terrible revenge on the user.

When I did, she whispered to me that they were waiting to bury the Five Clans in the jars and baskets at midnight during a full moon. In each container, the Five Clans would kill and eat one another until there was only one creature left. That one would be the strongest, most poisonous and most magical. When you dug it up, you could use it to work the old magic.

I remembered how fast the colonists' town had been destroyed. Even though it went against everything I had been taught, I was desperate enough to try anything. So I told Kumquat that I would help her when the moon was full.

I just hope the Dog Heads give us that much time.

Third month, nineteenth day

With the new disaster facing our tribe, Mother didn't get around to me until the next morning. From the tired expression on her face, I don't think she had gotten to sleep at all. That worried me so I suggested that she might want to take a nap first. She thought I was just trying to avoid punishment. Angrily she wanted to know what had possessed me to leave the village. I told her about my promise to the Chens. And I had done that, at least, for Madame. I told Mother that I had also saved some of the library as well. I thought of all the books I had to leave to the flames. And I felt as angry as I had for Father and for Master Chen.

Master Chen's books had opened up new worlds to me. They were like doorways across time and space. And the Dog Heads had contemptuously destroyed them. Saving the books was even more important than taking revenge. I think that's the last lesson Master Chen had been trying to teach me: Save the books for future generations.

Mother said that no matter how much good I had

done, it still did not justify leaving my post. If our people are to survive, we all must carry out our assignments.

I couldn't help pointing out that up to now the only job I had was sitting at home.

Mother said that was going to change right now. Great-Uncle Sambar had said I had handled myself well. And I had shown courage in saving the books.

That was high praise from Great-Uncle Sambar. It made me feel good but also a little scared. Was I going to be given some dangerous assignment like being a scout or spy?

I should have known Mother better. I was set to organizing the noncombatants!

Mother had also seen the chaos when the Chinese magistrate had come. We couldn't afford that when the Dog Heads finally attacked.

In other words, I was to be just a glorified nursemaid.

Then I remembered the town's wall. The elephants had tossed the logs aside like twigs.

When the elephants come, there will be no place to hide.

Whether I fought on the wall or hid in the palace, nowhere was safe.

Scroll five

Third Year of the Chung Ta T'ung Era
Third month, twentieth day to fourth
month, seventeenth day

Third month, twentieth day

Mother, Great-Uncle Sambar, and Little Tiger are in the next room. They're trying to come up with a plan that will save our people.

Little Tiger's all for meeting the Dog Heads in open battle.

Great-Uncle Sambar and Mother are trying to talk him out of his plan because we're no match for their war elephants.

His way will be a disaster, but my brother says that we can't stay in our villages. We'll be destroyed one by one like the colonists.

He thinks our courage will prevail even over elephants. He's no coward.

Mother's telling him that Father would not charge an elephant.

Little Tiger is boasting that he's braver than Father then.

And in the end, Mother and Great-Uncle Sambar must obey.

Whichever path we take — charge or hide — it leads to a dark and dismal end.

Hibiscus and Drongo are getting upset listening. I'll take them down to the riverbank to visit Father.

Later

The kingfisher eggs have hatched. Cheeping comes from almost every hole. It's loud enough to compete with the swollen river.

I think Father must be pleased.

We left him some treats and some coconut milk.

Then, as we stood there, we saw a flash of blue. It plunged like a dagger into the river. And the next moment a kingfisher arose with a silvery little fish wriggling in its beak.

It flew straight to a hole.

It made me think of how much I missed Father.

Drongo began to cry. He was worried about the babies. What would happen to them if the parents died?

I promised him that their big sister would take care of them.

I am concentrating on the task Mother gave me. If I stop to think, I'll become as anxious as Drongo.

I've gathered the children, the women, and the elderly in groups, and I've assigned them all to rally at the palace along certain streets. Hibiscus has a good head for detail and can keep track of who belongs to what team.

The warriors will have their own routes to their muster point so the two groups won't collide like last time.

At first, I wasn't sure the others would listen, especially the boys. However, there were no smirks. No insults. No pebbles thrown.

So after I had given the assignments, I called Barbet over and asked what was going on with the boys.

He said that word had gotten around about how I had plunged in and out of a burning house at the colonists' town.

I didn't think the others cared about books.

He said they didn't. But they could respect courage.

We ran through it most of the day until things went smoothly.

Still, it doesn't seem enough.

Poor Mother and Great-Uncle Sambar. There's so much else to be done. Little Tiger is practicing with the warriors. Not just archery and sword-fighting, though. They need to rehearse the signals of the bronze drum.

My brother has commanded that the one signal they will not practice is the one to retreat.

However, for all the glory on the battlefield, there are a lot of preparations that must be made in the background. And that's what Mother and Great-Uncle Sambar are doing.

With the colonists' town destroyed, there is no source of iron for weapons. We'll have to use bronze, which is softer. Worse, there's no salt to preserve fish and game to provide for the war band or to keep on hand should there be a siege of the town. Those are both problems as huge as the elephants. Of course, that's assuming we can stop those monsters that long.

Besides iron and salt, we won't be able to get candles, either. We will have to be careful with what we still have.

And we must have food. The council is gathering. Because the fields are lying idle, we will have no crops in the future. We must find substitutes somehow.

And there's a dozen other chores that the warriors need to do.

That's it!

We non-warriors can free the warriors to concentrating on fighting.

Third month, twenty-first day

I have organized some of the girls into squads and sent them through the village to gather every bronze pot, bowl, cup, and statue. Begonia was especially good at wheedling things from people. The bronze utensils can be melted down by the smiths for sword blades.

Even a weeping Toad surrendered the iron Chinese pots. I had never expected that since he had come to love them so.

The boys have been sent out to hunt. Even Drongo and Barbet have gone out, but I've seen that they each have an older boy as a partner. Both my brothers are under strict orders not to shoot their arrows if there's a remote chance there is a human in front of them.

I have also sent out other squads to gather the bamboo the warriors will need for arrow shafts, bows, and strings. Others will sort through bones from the debris pile for ones that can be shaped into arrowheads.

The smallest children are helping the elders. There are also jars of water to fill and store. There are nuts to find, and fruit has to be harvested from the fruit trees and dried. Vegetables need to be harvested. The forest must be scoured for edible food like tubers.

There's nothing I can do about the salt. However, we can preserve the fish and game by smoking it over low fires. The little children can help do that, too. They can gather fuel and feed the fires.

Barbet has a knack for machines. He and some of the older boys are repairing crossbows.

Third month, twenty-second day

It's begun to rain heavily again. We'll do our chores indoors. At the worst, we can sharpen bones into arrowheads.

I don't care if Peacock complains about the bone slivers messing up his floors.

Third month, twenty-third day

Little Tiger is meeting with the council, finally. Overhead the rain beats on the roof as if it were a great drum.

My brother had planned to discuss the assault on the Dog Heads, but lord Leopard of Big Rock insists that it is the Chinese, not the Dog Heads, who are the true threat. He still thinks we should buy the Dog Heads off. That way we'll be free to attack our real enemies, the Chinese, if they return to rebuild their colony.

Even with Mother's coaching, Little Tiger does not have Father's touch. Instead of reasoning with the great lords and elders of the council, he's trying to bully them like they're little brothers.

I think that's just the tantrum Lord Leopard has been waiting for. He is now insisting that Little Tiger is too young and inexperienced to lead the Hsien.

Oh, no, my brother is losing his temper.

He's playing into the hands of Big Rock. Lord Leopard is saying this proves that it should be Big Rock and not Kingfisher Hill that should lead the Hsien.

It's so easy to get my brother to fall into a trap.

That evening

What a catastrophe!

The council has broken up. It almost ended in a fist-fight. It might have been worse but Great-Uncle Sambar insisted everyone leave their weapons on the veranda outside the door.

Only half the Hsien have remained loyal — more for the sake of Father's memory than Little Tiger's own qualities. The other half are simply leaving, but at least they are not following Big Rock — as I think Lord Leopard expected them to do.

Little Tiger still thinks that when we sound the war drums that the Hsien will gather together. Great-Uncle Sambar, though, doesn't seem so sure.

I think they would have for Father. But they won't for my brother.

Late that evening

Mother found me crying by the shrine.

I told her that I miss Father.

She said that we all did. We all had to try to do our best without him.

I said that I didn't think Little Tiger was the one to lead us. He seemed to be trying to get all of us killed.

Mother says that Father casts a giant shadow. My big brother is just trying to prove himself.

I just hope it's not at our expense.

Third month, twenty-fourth day

It's still raining. However, I've checked my workers. Everything is coming along.

So I have time to think of what to do if Little Tiger's strategy fails.

I'll see if there's anything on elephants in the animal book.

There was an entire scroll on them. They've been used in war for a long time, though they are beginning to disappear from the southern forests.

However, the writer confirms that they're expensive to keep.

How are the Dog Heads paying for everything?

Of course. That's the point of the recent raids. And the attack on the silver mine must have gained them everything they needed.

The book doesn't have much to say about how to stop them, though. It just says that when an elephant is driven to panic it can be as dangerous to its friends as to its foes.

What could scare something that big?

Wait. I have another idea!

We can dig a wide ditch around the village and line the bottom and sides with thick, sharpened stakes.

That might help keep the elephants away. Hopefully archers on the walls can keep the Dog Heads from dumping dirt into the ditch and making a path for the elephants.

I'll go to Great-Uncle Sambar and Mother and suggest we do that.

They both think it's a good idea!

Now we just have to convince Little Tiger.

Later that day

My brother is more stubborn than a water buffalo. When he isn't practicing war, he's loafing around in his room with his friends from the Youth House. Because it's raining, they're staying inside the palace today.

It's noisy enough when my brothers and sisters play, but Little Tiger and his friends are ten times worse. It's hard to write.

He and his friends are convinced that Kingfisher Hill doesn't need the ditch. The men here are warriors. At least we got him to send messengers to suggest it to the other villages.

Third month, twenty-seventh day

Every scrap of metal has been rounded up. The warriors have plenty of supplies to use for arrows. And the food is piling up.

Since it stopped raining, I told the other children to

fetch the shovels and hoes from their houses. Then I led them outside. While they watched, I traced the ditch.

It's going to be awfully big.

I don't think children can dig something that large. But we have to try.

Later

We had barely scratched the ground when I heard Kumquat say that it was her turn.

I looked up to see my old nursemaid. And with her was her friend, Auntie Goral. And behind them were all the grandfathers and grandmothers and uncles and aunts.

They don't have much faith in my brother's scheme, either.

Though they're old, they're making the dirt fly.

Oh. Little Tiger's coming. He looks angry.

That afternoon

My brother's tried to order everyone back into the village. He's the king after all.

Kumquat said she won't take orders from someone whose bottom she used to spank.

To my surprise, Coconut, my brother's friend, set down his weapons. He stepped out from behind Little Tiger and said he'd take a turn. Then he took the shovel from his grandfather and began to dig.

That's made Little Tiger furious. However, Coconut went on shoveling away. He said he won't have his grandfather die of overwork.

One by one, the other warriors have taken the place of the elders. I guess we shamed them into digging the ditch.

Little Tiger glowered at everyone. And yet behind the angry face I thought I saw something else in his eyes. Fear.

So I walked over carefully to my brother. I think he expected me to humiliate him. However, I said to him strong warriors were good warriors. Digging the ditch and making stakes would build their muscles.

He glared at me for a moment but then he looked almost grateful for the excuse.

So he has sent off a group of men into the forest to cut down bamboo. At my suggestion they got a variety of thicknesses. Some we wanted strong enough to hold up against an elephant's hide or foot. Others we wanted smaller to keep out Dog Heads.

Third month, twenty-ninth day

It's been raining off and on. Work has become quite messy. The ditch became a small pond and the sides became muddy. Francolin has given up scolding me for getting dirty. She just rolls her eyes and asks heaven what she has done to be punished so.

Somehow the ditch got dug. We've sharpened the stakes that the men are setting in the bottom and sides. It's a thicket of points. It will be hard for a Dog Head, let alone an elephant, to get through.

That evening

It's raining again so Little Tiger and his fellow apes are inside. What a din!

Still, I feel good. Tonight Mother thanked me for being such a big help.

I told her it was the others who had done most of the work.

I can't stand the thought of being idle, however. There's too much time to get scared.

Somehow helping Kumquat feed her pets doesn't sound like enough.

There has to be something more we can all do if the Dog Heads come here.

I keep thinking of the colonists' town. I won't let that happen to Kingfisher Hill.

I just had the strangest dream. I must write it down while I still remember it. I lit one of my precious candles — even if it wakes up my little brothers and sisters.

I dreamed that I was stumbling through the forest trying to escape the Dog Heads. They were mounted on gray, monstrous elephants who trumpeted angrily. As fast as I ran, their elephants gained on me with long strides. Their huge bodies sent trees crashing out of their way.

And suddenly I came to a lake. Mist was rising from the surface. Out of the fog I saw a boat. As the water lapped at its side, I heard faint noises like distant thunder. From the lamp in the bow, I saw the gleam of fresh bronze.

I was frightened then. When I was small and acting up, Kumquat used to warn me that Ma Yüan would get me if I didn't behave. He was a Chinese general who had come from the north and crushed the free people, killing many and enslaving others. And he had taken their treasures, the great bronze drums, and melted them into huge columns as a monument to his conquests. And to this day, his ghost still haunts a lake to the west, traveling about in a boat of all bronze.

So I was sure it had to be the spirit of the terrible Ma Yüan. I wanted to run. Death at the hands of the Dog Heads would be preferable to that awful phantom.

However, my legs were paralyzed. I could only stand helplessly as the ship crew closer. And behind me I heard the Dog Heads and their elephants closing in.

But instead of Ma Yüan, I saw Master Chen upon the deck of the boat. He was in his teacher's robe and cap, and he was smiling. When he held out his hand, a metal plank from the boat was thrust onto the shore.

Suddenly, I could move again and I found myself walking up the plank. When I took Master Chen's hand, he began to glow, and the light spread outward. I felt my body tingle with it, and the brightness went right through our feet and into the boat until it glowed bright as a paper lantern.

And the sails stretched and stretched until they became great wings. As they beat the air, the boat began to rise above the mist. However, the boat didn't escape into the air. Instead, it hovered, beating at the fog that began to stretch out in tendrils. And the streamers took shape, becoming snakes and pincers and fangs. They reached out, wrapping and grabbing the Dog Heads.

The Dog Heads began to scream in fear and the elephants went wild with terror. But the mists covered them and then it was silent.

I turned to Master Chen to thank him, but he was gone. And I was alone on the boat, gliding through the air.

And then I awoke.

Mother's stirring, so I should stop now.
Perhaps it's an omen?

Fourth month, first day

I've asked Kumquat what she thinks the dream meant.
She and Auntie Goral and the other old women are getting ready to bury the jars soon. And she said it was a sign that we would win. She's sure that it meant the old magic would destroy our enemies.

In the light of day, though, I have less faith in my dream. A sharp arrow is more dependable.

Later

A band of warriors have arrived from our neighboring village to the south. They will be the first of many for the great hosting.

We have more than enough food for the war band. However, Little Tiger has panicked and ordered everyone in the village to help make extra provisions. There was food to be smoked or pickled, jars to be made, and baskets to be woven. We are to work night and day. There will be no time to perform the old magic.

Poor Kumquat and the other aunties are beside themselves. I just hope they don't hex my brother.

Warriors have been gathering despite the steady rain. They're camped now all around Kingfisher Hill. They're even in the fields we have not been able to plant. The rains have turned the ground into sticky mud.

In all the commotion, no one but me has noticed all the little old grannies and aunties are also gathering. They bring with them jars. I bet people assume it's food. I know better, though.

It's good that we built up our reserves to feed them all.

My brother keeps asking me what I think of this warrior or that. At first, I thought he was simply teasing. Now I'm beginning to think he's trying to make a match.

I'll pick my own husband, thank you.

I wish Kumquat would stop singing her love songs and then rolling hey eyes at me meaningfully. When I glare at her, she just grins. Worse, Hibiscus and Begonia have picked up the habit, too.

And Mother is constantly sending me back to my room to comb my hair or put on better clothes. She never used to worry about my appearance before.

If I didn't love them, I could choke them all.

Late afternoon

At last! It's stopped raining.

Kumquat and Francolin are busy with loads of laundry. Now is a chance to wash and dry things.

Everywhere people are outside enjoying the sun.

I took Barbet and the others down to visit Father. Then I held onto them while they peered down the riverbank. The fledglings were just emerging from their nests and trying their wings.

They seemed so surprised that they can move through the air — though maybe I shouldn't call it flying. It's more like flopping from one spot in the sky to another.

That night

Not much time to write. Little Tiger is entertaining the lords and Mother and I are busy serving.

There are many calls for Mother to play the drums. She says her drumming days are done. And I —

What's that noise?

Later that night

Mother and I went out to find Coconut and all of Little Tiger's Ape House friends stumbling out of the palace.

Some of them didn't even bother to climb down the ladder but jumped.

And Little Tiger was chasing them, waving Father's ax.

I was just standing there with my mouth open when Mother shoved me hard from behind. I fell forward in front of Little Tiger's legs. The next moment I was flat on the floor with Little Tiger on top of me. And I could hear Mother telling him to calm down.

When I squirmed out from under my brother, I saw she had grabbed his arms from behind. As she gripped him, she demanded to know what was wrong.

"Look what Coconut did to Father's ax!" he moaned.

By the light of the Chinese candles, I saw a small nick in the edge. It seems that Coconut had chopped at a small stone statue in the room.

I told him that when the ax was sharpened the nick would disappear.

That seemed to calm him down. He examined the ax again and announced that he was through with those idiots. They couldn't be trusted to take anything seriously. They acted like he was still in the Youth House with them.

I would have said the same about my brother, but I held my tongue.

Mother let go of him and told him that he'd had to

grow up faster than they did. They just didn't realize it yet. But they would soon.

Little Tiger rested his head on her shoulder as if he were a small boy. He hadn't known it would be so hard. He wished Father was still alive so he didn't have to do this. He knew he was doing a miserable job.

Mother said some soothing things to him. I just stared. So this was the bold warrior king. Inside, he was just as frightened as I was.

I thought of the fledgling kingfishers I had seen this afternoon. They were probably just as scared when they tried their wings.

Suddenly, Little Tiger became aware of me sitting there watching him. He sat up with a start and forbade me to tell anyone.

I told him that I didn't need any such order. This was a family matter and such things stayed within the palace.

He still looked suspicious and resentful. Rubbing his head, he said he wished he had not wasted the time when he had lived in the palace. He could have eavesdropped from another room as I did. He'd always found it boring and used to skip out as soon as the discussions started. He added that I had probably listened to more of them than he had.

That was the truth, but I tried to be nice and say he

seemed to have learned something because no one was complaining.

He shook his head. People keep expecting answers, he said, but his mind feels like an empty jar. It was all a performance like a Chinese actor. And it didn't help that I keep undermining his authority.

I demanded to know how I had done that.

He said I kept making fun of him. The latest incident was with the ditch.

I argued that I was only following Mother's and Great-Uncle Sambar's advice.

That didn't make my brother feel any better. He knew the idea had come from me because Coconut had heard others talking. He was a fake king. Everyone in the village knew he was a mindless fool. He was sure they were laughing behind his back.

I'd never seen my brother like this. All the swagger and strut was gone. He was like a rooster that had lost his tail.

Fortunately, I remembered what Mother had said about my brother trying to live in my father's shadow.

Being king was a lonely job, and I said so. I hadn't meant to make things harder.

The old Little Tiger would have used that as an excuse to hit me. This was a newer one, though. He just stared at me as he set the ax down on the floor.

Gently, Mother told him that not even Father had known all the answers. Being king did not mean you suddenly knew everything. The job was so big that it was the reverse. It made you realize how little you understood. That's why Father had found people whose advice he trusted. And he hadn't been afraid to ask for it in public.

Little Tiger took a deep breath and then let it out in a deep sigh. He thanked Mother. And he said tomorrow he'd thank Great-Uncle Sambar. And then he turned to me and actually thanked me.

I was glad I was sitting down or I would have fallen over in shock.

fourth month, eleventh day

My brother's like a new man. He keeps Great-Uncle Sambar by his side and asks him what to do. And at meals, my brother hardly touches the wine.

He just might make a good king, and —

I hear thunder in the distance. Is it a storm?

No, it's the drums, carrying a message across the Great Forest:

The Dog Heads are coming!

This is my first chance to write. I'm exhausted but too excited and too scared to nap like the others.

It's Big Rock that's in trouble. Lord Leopard is begging us for help. I guess they found out the hard way that you can't bargain with the Dog Heads.

So far they've held off the Dog Heads and their elephants. Maybe they dug their own ditch.

Little Tiger thinks this is our chance. If the war band moves quickly, we can surprise the Dog Heads. They won't be expecting a swift attack from their rear. Or at least we'll catch them between us and Big Rock.

And Great-Uncle Sambar agrees.

The whole village was in an uproar as the great war band got ready to leave. Everyone was rushing this way and that.

And then my brother strode out onto the veranda, Father's ax in his hand. He looked every ch'ih the king.

Uncle Muntjac was waiting for him at the foot of the ladder. He begged to go. Little Tiger, however, told him he's needed here.

"You mean I'm a useless old fool," Uncle Muntjac said and sank down and began to weep. He was wailing that he should never have come back from the ambush. Everyone thought he was a coward for surviving when all of his comrades had died.

I tried to comfort him as I passed, but he just shook his head, crawled under his house, and sat among the pigs.

Mother, myself, and the other brothers and sisters followed Little Tiger through the village. Everywhere people were cheering.

Great-Uncle Sambar was waiting by the gates. And waiting behind him was the war band. I had never seen so many people gathered together, not even in the colonists' town. Even though this was only part of the Hsien's strength, surely it will be enough to sweep the Dog Heads back into their mountains.

I cheered from the palisade with everyone else.

That afternoon

Uncle Muntjac isn't the only one who's upset. When I went home to rest, I found Kumquat in a corner rocking back and forth and groaning.

She should have gone ahead with what she had at the last full moon. But she had been waiting to gather more of the Five Clans. Now it's too late.

Fourth month, thirteenth day

Uncle Muntjac is still under his house with his pigs. But I think I have an idea to get him out. I just have to get the other children to help me. We'll form our own little "army."

Later

Drongo and Barbet actually like the idea of having our own war band! And they've convinced the other children that we can help man the palisade.

I've told everyone to bring a bow and arrows to the palace.

That afternoon

We went over to Uncle Muntjac's house. He was still hiding underneath there with each arm around a pig. I got on all fours and crept over to him.

I asked him to help us sharpen our archery skills.

That perked Uncle Muntjac up. He —

He's shouting at me to stop writing and get back to target practice.

The old warrior is back to his old self.

Fourth month, fourteenth day

Still no word from Little Tiger. Mother paces back and forth.

Everyone, down to the smallest baby, is nervous.

Kumquat mopes around.

What are we going to do with all her poisonous pets? It's not like we can turn them loose all together.

Fourth month, seventeenth day

Disaster!

The first stragglers have come back. The war band walked straight into an ambush. The Dog Heads were waiting. And the warriors from Big Rock were standing by their side.

Now we know who betrayed Father.

It wasn't the Chinese. It was Big Rock.

They've always wanted to regain the leadership of the Hsien. They couldn't get the other villages to support their claims so they struck a deal with our enemies. They eliminated Father and tried to put the blame on the Chinese. That way they thought they could regain leadership of the Hsien and send us off to weaken ourselves by battling the colonists.

Since that plan failed, Big Rock and the Dog Heads

will simply destroy Kingfisher Hill, and then Big Rock will use the Dog Heads to conquer the rest of the Hsien.

Scum.

No, that's an insult to scum. They are lower than scum.

And Big Rock's leaders are foolish. What makes them think the Dog Heads will turn over Hsien territory to them once they're in control?

But we won't be alive to see them get their own rewards.

I have to stop writing now. Drongo and Hibiscus are crying.

Must get them to stop before they set of Begonia and Barbet. Mother has to concentrate on the stragglers and find out what happened. But this first bunch must have thrown their weapons away and run the first chance they got. So they don't know anything. They were too busy running.

I can't condemn them, though. I think I would have fled, too.

That evening

Survivors have been trickling in all day.

The war band fought bravely, and no one was braver than Little Tiger. But what could he do against elephants? It was a horrible slaughter.

Even so, my brother tried to rally the war band for one more charge. However, Great-Uncle Sambar told him to retreat and save what he could.

At first, he didn't want to do that, saying it was the coward's way out.

However, Great-Uncle Sambar said saving the war band was more important than salvaging his pride.

I think Little Tiger is growing as a ruler. He saw the sense in that and ordered the war band to retreat. They say he was the last to leave the battlefield.

No one can doubt his courage. Or that of our warriors. They have made the Dog Heads pay a high price.

Our enemies did not pursue. They're sitting at Big Rock licking their wounds.

Later that evening

We've had word from Little Tiger and Great-Uncle Sambar.

Tonight they've regrouped the survivors of the war band. They expect Big Rock and the Dog Heads to follow soon. To get to our village, the Dog Heads must cross the mountains of Cinnamon Pass. In that narrow valley, the Dog Head's numbers won't count as much, nor will the elephants be so devastating a weapon.

Little Tiger might even have a chance to stop them if it

weren't for the elephants. At least they'll try to slow them down as much as they can.

In the meantime, we are to evacuate the ancient grottoes and store up supplies there.

From the pass, Little Tiger will fall back to Kingfisher Hill and join us in the grottoes.

Later

I can't sleep so I've gotten up to write. Somehow it doesn't matter if I waste a precious candle now. In a few days, Kingfisher Hill may be a ruin just like Kao-liang.

And —

Mother's crying.

This all I can write for now. I have to see what's wrong.

Later

I'm sorry about my handwriting, but my hand's trembling. I was shaken by seeing Mother weep. She's always so strong. My rock.

She was trying so hard not to wake the little ones. But the tears kept flowing down her cheeks.

I watched over her until she fell asleep. Then I lay down, too, but sleep won't come. I can hear little bodies breathing. My brothers and sisters trust me. That's why they can rest so deeply. I've promised them they'll be safe.

And I think of all the other sleeping people in the village. They trust us, too.

But what can we do?

It all comes down to stopping the elephants. Maybe we can buy off the Chams who guide the elephants. No, the Dog Heads have all the silver from the mine.

The Chams are mercenaries, though. They have no grudge against us to keep on fighting. Their main interest will be in protecting themselves and their animals. We wouldn't have to kill all the elephants. Just a few. And that would be enough to discourage the Chams. I will bet anything that they would withdraw then.

But killing a single war elephant seems just as impossible as destroying them all.

How? How? How?

I feel like Little Tiger. I keep searching for answers. But it's like putting my hand into an empty jar. There's nothing. *Nothing.*

I'm going for a walk. Soon we'll have to begin the evacuation.

Scroll Six

Third Year of the Chung Ta T'ung Era
fourth month, eighteenth to
twenty-ninth day

I have it! I think I know how to stop the Dog Heads.

When I left the palace, there was a low fog on the ground. It was as if the village was riding on a cloud.

Then, in the midst of that lonely scene, I heard someone singing under her breath about a boy who loved his buffalo better than her. The lament was one of Kumquat's favorites.

And then my old nursemaid came shuffling around a corner, kicking up wisps of fog. She has rheumatism, so the damp cold made it painful to walk. With her were Auntie Goral and all the other old grannies and aunties.

When I asked her what they was doing up so early, she grumbled that she was going to start evacuating the "pets." If they didn't start taking them to the caves now, she knew they would be left behind.

With a little luck, we could hold off the Dog Heads until the old folk can save all of us with the old magic.

I tried to convince them all to go back and rest. We

would have enough work moving the animals and food stores into the caves.

However, Kumquat scolded me, saying that I, above all people, should believe in the old magic. Didn't my dream prophesy that the old magic would save us?

The dream.

I looked out at the fog. As I took a step, ribbons of mist rose. I chopped at them with my arm and watched them writhe like snakes.

I felt an idea teasing my mind just like one of those misty serpents.

Since Kumquat was so determined, I told her that I'd help. She leaned on me as we went to the first of the storage sheds.

When she opened the door, the pungent odor of cinnamon rolled around me. I would have sworn I was in the forest in Cinnamon Pass. But instead of fragrant trees, I was surrounded by hissing jars.

And then I had it.

I thought of how the elephants had panicked in my dream when the mist snakes had coiled around them. I remembered Master Chen's animal book again. It said that frightened elephants could be as much a danger to their friends as their enemies.

And that was it.

Kumquat was so startled when I hugged her. I would have danced around if her tender joints hadn't been hurting her. So I told her to feed her pets. Get them good and fat.

Then I went back and woke Mother.

The Dog Heads will be expecting us to oppose them at Cinnamon Pass.

But we can pull off an ambush of our own. We might not be able to cause panic in the elephants directly, but we could cause panic in the Chams who were guiding them.

I thought of the trees in the narrow pass again. The branches overhung the floor of the pass. The thick canopy of branches was like a roof. From those branches, we can drop the jars right on top of the elephants.

Once their drivers are distracted, we might be able to upset the elephants in turn.

At the very least, they could cause some damage among the Dog Heads and the traitors of Big Rock.

I wish you could have seen the old women's faces when I told them we wouldn't have to wait until the full moon to use the Five Clans.

It was like throwing twigs onto the hearth coals. I could see the fire springing up in their eyes.

Kumquat was all for setting out then and there.

If it was just a question of determination, I know that she and the other women could do it. Their hearts are young but not their legs. And that's what I told them. Mother could send a group with the jars to the pass instead.

Kumquat shook her head sadly. She was sure Mother would never let anyone else leave for Cinnamon Pass. Instead, she would want all hands to help with evacuating to the grottoes. And without Mother's orders, none of the younger adults will help.

Of course, I should not deceive Mother. However, I have no choice. Thank heaven that I have my own little war band now.

I'm scared of the elephants, but there's no choice.

I know it's only a faint chance. But Little Tiger needs every bit of help that he can get.

Later

I'm so proud of my little warriors.

With the help of Kumquat and the grannies and aunties, I roused them without waking up the other adults. Then I made my proposal to them. There was some gulping. No one in their right mind would want to take on a war elephant.

However, every one of them volunteered.

The younger ones like Drongo and Hibiscus can't go, of course. Their legs are too short. So they are to make excuses for the others. For instance, when Mother asks for me, Drongo can say that he just saw me but I went to help so-and-so. In a short time, it will be hectic in the village. In the confusion, it will be hard to keep track of the children. That should gain us some time so we can put some distance between us and Kingfisher Hill.

Later

We nearly had another disaster. Uncle Muntjac caught us raiding the storage sheds for meat jerky and other supplies.

He thinks our plan is crazy. He was going to wake Mother and tell her.

However, I stopped him and I pointed out that we'd have no means of escape in the grottoes. The Dog Heads could wait for us to run out of food. The place to stop the Dog Heads is at the pass, not at Kingfisher Hill or our grottoes. If he had a better scheme to stop them there, I was willing to listen.

Uncle Muntjac doesn't. But he still doesn't want us to go. At least in the grottoes, some of us might survive.

I told Uncle Muntjac that I was disappointed in him. I always thought of him as a true warrior, and I never thought he was a coward.

He straightened as if he had just stepped on a scorpion

himself. He wanted me, his princess, alive, not dead. And dead I would be if I went to the pass.

Kumquat told him that I might survive if I stayed in the caves, but it would be as the slave of the Dog Heads. The war band had eaten up most of our reserves. We couldn't stand a long siege. It was either win at the pass or lose in the grottoes.

He thought a moment and then grabbed a carrying band. If I was set on going, he would go with me and keep me alive as long as he could.

The bulk of our load will be the Five Clans.

Kumquat and the other old women are determined to go as far as they can. They'll carry the food for our pets. Can't have them dying before we meet the elephants. As they empty their jars of pet food, they'll turn back.

We'll match our tiny pets against the Dog Heads' big ones. And we'll see who wins.

Later that morning
En route to Cinnamon Pass

I have to make this quick. This is only a short stop. We have to put as much distance as we can between ourselves and Kingfisher Hill. We don't want Mother catching us.

I told the sentries we were taking supplies to the caves

and they let us out of the gates. With invaders coming, they didn't stop to ask why we were leaving armed with all the bows, arrows, and knives we could carry.

Then we headed in the direction of the river-crossing to the grottoes. However, once we were out of sight, we headed for the pass instead.

So far, no pursuit.

It's the first time I used a carrying band. It is slung over your forehead, supporting the weight of the jar on your back. But my neck is already aching.

And it gives me the shivers to hear things slithering and rattling around inside the jar. My pets sound furious.

Good.

They can take out their anger on our enemies.

That afternoon

Because of the load and the age of some of my companions, we have not made much progress.

Some of the older women are already going to have to drop out. They'll make their way back to the village after resting.

I didn't eat much. I was hungry enough, at first, but I lost my appetite as soon as Kumquat and the other old women began to feed the Five Clans.

Curious. Uncle Muntjac is just as squeamish as me about insects and snakes.

But my little sister, Begonia, is fascinated by them. I think Kumquat's found an apprentice.

And —

Later

Sorry for the interruption.

I had to stop Kumquat from tormenting Uncle Muntjac. She took out a scorpion — she knows how to hold them so she doesn't get stung. And then she started to chase Uncle Muntjac around our camp.

There he was, this old, tough warrior, screaming at her to keep away. However, he couldn't go too fast because of his bad leg. Fortunately, Kumquat wasn't any faster because of her rheumatism.

The sight was so comical we all rolled on the ground with laughter. Finally, I brushed away the tears. It was good to remember what it was like to laugh again — if only for a moment. And then I went to Uncle's rescue.

Kumquat said she was getting even for all the times Uncle used to tease her when they were both small children.

Uncle, of course, doesn't remember.

Kumquat just wishes she had known about his fear of

crawling creatures back then. Her childhood would have been a lot happier if she could have stopped him from bullying her.

That evening

I am writing this by the light of a campfire.

Kumquat and Uncle Muntjac have grown quite chummy. They're giggling and teasing each other like children.

They'll get along if Kumquat doesn't pull out another scorpion.

And as long as she has a jar of crawling creatures available, Uncle will be sure to behave himself.

So will Barbet, for that matter. Begonia has copied Kumquat and is tormenting her brother with bugs.

Fourth month, nineteenth day

We came upon the first of the war band today. These frightened, hunted men look a far cry from the bold warriors who marched away from Kingfisher Hill.

We shared some of our supplies with them and they ate like they were starving tigers.

They think we're taking supplies to the pass. So they warned us not to stay long. They quake at the very mention of elephants. The Chams have taught their beasts to trample people on command. And when the elephants swing their heads, the sharp blades tied to their tusks can cut a man in two.

All of these men are our former allies. They're disobeying Little Tiger. As soon as they take our wounded to our village, they're not staying. They're heading to their homes to do what they can to defend them. I guess I can't blame them.

That evening

We met stragglers the whole day. Our supplies are shrinking as we share what we have with them.

The once great war band has become a bunch of scared men fleeing for their lives.

Their fear is catching.

Fourth month, twentieth day

Too tired to write much. The pace has been hard. I'd say over half the old women have had to drop out.

Kumquat is trying her best, but she can't keep up. She falls behind quickly and only catches up when we've stopped for a rest.

The funny thing is that Uncle Muntjac keeps her company. They are an odd, but admirable, couple.

Fourth month, twenty-first day

We made it.

I can smell the cinnamon trees, though I can't see them.

All of our stomachs are rumbling because we've run out of food. Our pets are better off.

I have to hand it to Kumquat and the old women. Half of them have managed to keep up with us.

Have to stop now.

Uncle Muntjac wants to sort his little army into a column like the Chinese militia used to form. He doesn't want us to look like a mob.

Poor Uncle Muntjac. He's like a gnat trying to keep a herd of water buffalo in order. The women, led by Kumquat, are giving him the worst time.

I better give him a hand — before they make him cry.

Later

Well, the column collapsed into a straggling crowd as soon as we started off again. Uncle Muntjac's growling that he'd rather face a horde of Dog Heads than a pack of old women. However, I think that he enjoys being teased by the women, especially Kumquat — though he would never admit it.

From our resting place, I can see the trees dotting the pass. Axes thud in the distance.

And there's an ape hooting. Except this ape sounds familiar. I —

Later

It's Coconut. He dropped out of the trees. He's standing sentry duty.

I was surprised he would be posted even in the rear.

Coconut said that Little Tiger had learned to be cautious. It has been an expensive lesson.

I'm glad that Coconut's life wasn't part of the price. He can be annoying at times, but I've gotten used to him.

But he looks so grim now. It makes him look far older than he is.

That evening
Cinnamon Pass

My plan won't work! All that effort. All that hope. Wasted.

We've reached the war band. What's left of it. They have only half their strength. The losses are either casualties or deserters.

They've built a wall of trees across the floor of the pass! And they've dug a ditch in front of it and put in stakes.

But to build all that, they cut down the trees all around the wall. There's a huge hole in the tree canopy. I can see the sky now. We have no way of dropping the jars on the elephants.

Even so, despite all their efforts the wall only goes partway up on either side. The Dog Heads can still sweep around it. There aren't enough of our warriors to hold the pass, brave as they are.

As soon as they saw the gap in the tree canopy, my little group knew we had already failed. We just stopped as a group and sank to our knees.

It was a fool's errand to come up here. I look at my little band of warriors. The old people and children are sleeping where they first sat down. They're so exhausted.

Have I led them on a mad march?

That's what I get for listening to everyone say how clever I am. I actually started to believe it. However, I was just grasping at a crazy dream this time.

I feel like crying. But I mustn't. Not in front of everyone. They still look up to me, even though I'm an idiot.

I'm such a fool!

First, Great-Uncle Sambar gave me a lecture.

Then he led me over to Little Tiger. My brother has bandages on his arm and around his head. Even so, he was cutting down a tree with Father's war ax. It's not really the proper tool for chopping wood, but it's all he has.

I'd never seen him do manual labor before, but everyone has to help with the defenses.

Little Tiger's furious with me. The scouts say the Dog Heads are finally about to move out of Big Rock. Old people and children have no place on a battlefield. This is no game to pass the time in the village. This is real war. He has already seen too many people die.

His concern surprised me and I thanked him.

He actually apologized then! He doesn't want my last memory of him to be harsh.

Despite the plan he had sent to Mother, he does not expect to live through the next battle.

He looks so much older now. And his mouth is as grim as Coconut's.

That made me feel even worse, and I began to cry. I thought I had a way to save him, but it is useless now.

Great-Uncle Sambar demanded to know what my

scheme had been. I told him that we could have turned the Dog Heads' strength into weakness.

Little Tiger has changed — or he is desperate. Instead of dismissing my idea outright, he asked me what I had expected to do. How could a war band of children and elderly women stop war elephants when our bravest warriors couldn't?

I said that was the point. The war elephants were such a mighty weapon that no one thought of anything else. We were terrified of the huge beasts. And the Dog Heads put all their faith and confidence into those same monstrous animals. If we were to stop even some of the elephants, the Dog Heads might lose their taste for a battle. However, Little Tiger had our war band cut down the trees, which spoiled all my plans.

Great-Uncle Sambar said they had to clear the area so the Dog Heads had no cover in front of the wall. Of course, Little Tiger demanded to know how trees could stop the elephants.

So I opened the lid of my jar.

Right away, I had to slam it down because a snake tried to get out.

Little Tiger jumped back like a giant flea.

Despite my disappointment, I had to smile. The Cham mercenaries would have acted just the same way if the venomous snakes and insects could have dropped on them from above.

Great-Uncle Sambar looked very thoughtful. He said it was hard to hit an elephant when it was going fast.

I told him that I had figured that out, too. If we pulled up ropes at the height of the elephant drivers, they would have to slow down or be knocked off.

Great-Uncle Sambar slapped his thighs and roared with laughter. All the warriors turned around, startled. I don't think there's been any laughter in the war band since the battle at Big Rock.

Little Tiger says that I'm good at outsmarting people. So he's glad to have me planning against the Dog Heads rather than against him.

They've borrowed my jar and gone off with the remaining lords. They're talking right now, and I'm taking the opportunity to bring the history up to date.

Little Tiger's right.

War isn't a game to amuse children.

Before this, I was too busy with plans and carrying them out. But now that I have a chance to think about things, I realize that people will actually die. I think I've been too clever for my own good.

Oh, here comes Great-Uncle Sambar and Little Tiger. I'm probably in for a scolding.

Midnight

I'm writing this by the light of a campfire. I should be sleeping but I'm too excited.

Little Tiger still has some doubts about my scheme, but they have little choice.

He and Great-Uncle Sambar, however, have changed my plan a little.

The trees may be gone from in front of the wall, but there are plenty of trees behind it.

Great-Uncle Sambar says the trick is to funnel the Dog Heads and elephants and Big Rock warriors into the pass.

Half of the war band will wait a little way behind the wall. The defenders will fight at the wall but then pretend to panic. They'll fool the Dog Heads into thinking they have us on the run. That way they won't bother to move up on the sides of the pass.

The Dog Heads will probably attack the wall with the war elephants first. So we will leave the ditch unfinished and maybe take out some of the stakes. That way it won't be a real obstacle to the huge beasts. When they break through, the war elephants will lead the pursuit as they did at Big Rock. The animals' long strides should outstrip the Dog Heads and the Big Rock warriors so Little Tiger and his war band will lead them farther down the pass to an area where the trees have not been cut yet.

Then we'll spring our trap.

We'll use a spiderweb of ropes. They won't stop an elephant, but they could knock a man off the elephant's back. We'll put the ropes up at about the right height in front and behind.

The Chams will have to stop long enough to tear down the ropes. That should allow our people in the tree branches time enough to aim and drop the jars. We'll rain poisonous snakes and bugs down on those killers.

Hopefully, some of the elephants will panic. Great-Uncle Sambar will be waiting with the war band stationed on either side of the pass, hidden in the trees. They'll charge down. It will be our best chance to kill some of the beasts. If we even slay a few, the Chams might get discouraged and retreat. And when they see the powerful war elephants withdrawing, the Dog Heads will fall back, as well.

As I'm describing the plan here, I realize it's a lot of maybes. But what choice do we have?

It's all about gaining time. Bloody the noses of the Dog Heads and make them hesitate.

That will allow Mother to gather more supplies for a siege in the grottoes. And perhaps it will even let her rally the rest of the Hsien. The treachery of Big Rock is clear to everyone now. And who could stay neutral with the Dog Heads invading?

If we can hold Cinnamon Pass, we may yet save Kingfisher Hill and the Hsien.

Fourth month, twenty-fourth day

I've hardly had time to sit and think — let alone write. I'm having some water and dried jujubes. So much to do.

Work has stopped on the wall. I'm directing the other children to filling in part of the ditch — we don't want to discourage the elephants after all.

That leaves the warriors free to cut down bamboo. We'll need lots.

You cut the bamboo lengthwise over and over until you have long, thin strips. Then you braid them into rope. It's actually stronger than rope made from other fibers. We'll loop them over branches at the proper height. And at the proper time, we'll pull them taut so they'll be at the level of the Cham drivers.

Wait. There's another problem. If Great-Uncle Sambar is going to charge the elephants, what will they do about all the venomous snakes and insects under foot?

Later

I have it. There are a lot of hides lying around the war band's camp. They are left over from game or stray buffalo that had wandered into the pass that have been killed to feed the warriors.

From them, we can fashion shoes and boots like the Chinese wear. They'll be crude, but they should serve the purpose. Barbet and Begonia can take over for me while I fashion a pair.

Later

Little Tiger has tried on the first pair. They are big and clumsy because I didn't have the time to cut them to the proper size — or the cobbler's skill to do it right. He has to walk in a high-stepping stomp. He says it makes him walk like an elephant.

Kumquat and the older folk can take over work on the shoes. And the children can help when they're finished with the ditch.

To be sure that the Dog Heads don't see our preparations, Great-Uncle Sambar had spread out a wide net of skirmishers.

Later

Uncle Muntjac and the aunties have been hiding the jars up into the trees. It will be a chore to feed the Five Clans, but we may not have time to put them up there when the

Dog Heads arrive. I expect the insect-loving Begonia will be good at climbing up and feeding our pets.

I was surprised when Uncle Muntjac slung a jar on his back and then began to climb up a big tree himself. He says he used to be a regular monkey.

Kumquat made a rude noise, saying that Uncle Muntjac was getting so old he was forgetting everything. She had been the champion of Kingfisher Hill. And despite her rheumatic legs, she climbed up a neighboring tree and stored a jar away.

I'm sure they'll both feel it later, though. I just hope Kumquat packed some of her salve for their aching knees.

Of course, I had to take a jar up myself. I went higher than I had ever been before. When I had wedged the jar securely in a fork of the tree, I gazed around me.

It was strange to be so far above the ground. All the preparations for war were only distant sounds. People and their problems looked so small from high in the sky.

It was so peaceful among the branches that I could almost forget we were at war. It was like floating in a pond of drifting weeds.

And then I heard a rattling in the jar. I think some scorpions were fighting. So we had brought war even to the treetops now. This is where I'll fight. I squinted down, picturing an elephant and a Cham beneath me. We are all going to bring our weapons up into the trees, too.

I thought about shooting a Cham or Dog Head with an arrow. I had told Great-Uncle Sambar I would. But could I really?

Suddenly, I heard a rustle in the green canopy around me. Startled, I twisted around in time to see a flash of red. And then I heard a birdcall.

I crept along the branch until I could peer through a small gap in the canopy. I was just in time to see a redbird spiral upward toward the sun.

Kumquat would have called it a good omen.

All it did was make me think of Master Chen.

I'm doing my best, I whispered to him.

I have to finish now. I want to find a hollow tree where I can leave my history. Perhaps it will survive even if I don't.

fourth month, twenty-fifth day
Afternoon

This is terribly embarrassing!

I had written a wonderfully grand speech to give before the battle. It was based on the speeches of famous Chinese generals from the history books. I think at least Uncle Muntjac and Kumquat would have sat through it. But I'm going to have to forget it.

Great Warriors do not have their mothers order them home from the battlefield.

Peacock reached us last evening. He was footsore and exhausted because he's used to life in the palace. However, he panted out Mother's command: We are to return to Kingfisher Hill in no uncertain terms. No excuses. No delays.

I tried to hint to Little Tiger that he was the king and not Mother. However, Little Tiger just laughed at me. Even he knows better than to cross her at certain times. And this was one of them.

So I had to fetch my history from the tree where I had hidden it.

At the moment, we're taking a short break on the way back home. Everyone looks gloomy. We all know what's waiting for us back at home. Scoldings. Spankings. And plenty of punishment chores. And this time I don't think Mother will let me write my history as my penalty.

It's only the children, though. Barbet and Begonia are both pouting.

Kumquat and the old women refused to go. Someone has to tend our little pets. And what does it take to drop a jar from a tree? They can take the place of warriors who should be fighting on the ground.

Peacock insisted that it was my mother's order that everyone return.

Kumquat just laughed. What was the queen mother

going to do to her old nursemaid? Auntie Goral and the other old women do not seem scared, either.

Poor old Uncle Muntjac was torn. On the one hand, he has sworn to protect me. On the other hand, I think he also wants to guard Kumquat.

So I leaned in close and asked him in a whisper to watch over my old nursemaid as a favor to me.

He was glad for the excuse.

Kumquat was flustered when he announced he was going to stay. She knows everything about love — but only when it's for someone else.

She insisted his place was beside me.

However, I said that the war band would need every warrior it could find.

Little Tiger isn't such a fool as I thought, either. He's seen how close Kumquat and Uncle Muntjac have become. So he ordered Uncle Muntjac to stay, saying that he would answer to Mother later.

I couldn't resist humming Kumquat's favorite love song back to her. Revenge is so sweet!

Then we left the old couple together, blushing like two children.

As we were getting ready to go, Coconut came over to me. He shuffled his feet and looked awkward. I assumed he wanted me to run some errand for him back in Kingfisher Hill.

I was feeling a bit testy about leaving the battlefield. What was the point of all that archery practice and planning?

I feel as if I'm running away.

So I'm afraid I was a bit short with him. I said to tell me what he wanted and to be quick about it.

I was surprised when he pulled a huge orchid from behind his back. I know they grow only at the very top of the higher trees where the monkeys alone risk climbing.

I thought he wanted me to give it to his mother, but I was shocked when he said it was for me. In a rush, he said he hoped he could come courting when this is all over.

Strange.

He's always treated me like such a pest before this.

I'm sure when Coconut comes back he'll just say the orchid was a joke.

I should throw it away before I feel like a fool. But I can't for some reason.

It's getting crushed inside my clothes. I guess I'll put it my hair.

I don't care how much the others tease me.

fourth month, twenty-sixth day
Morning
four li from Cinnamon Pass

The war drums are booming and the horns are sounding from the pass. Or is it the elephants stomping and trumpeting?

I've sent Peacock back to the pass to check. In the meantime, we'll wait where we are. There's no way we can reach Kingfisher Hill if the Dog Heads break through. We'll have to scatter into the forest and hope we can hide from them.

I look at my little war band. They all are so young. They have followed me here because they trusted me.

What have I gotten them into?

That evening

Peacock's come back. We've won! A great victory!

Barbet and Begonia and I and everyone else have danced ourselves silly.

Nothing really went as planned, but I guess nothing ever does in war. The elephants and Dog Heads stormed the wall together. They struck with such fury that it was all Little Tiger could do to retreat.

And the Dog Heads kept so close on his heels that they were mixed with his rearguard. Our warriors were afraid

233

to spring the trap because it would have caught Little Tiger and many of his men.

It was Coconut who rallied a group of warriors, many of them from the Ape House. He led them in a desperate charge at the Dog Heads and the elephants. It was so outrageous that our enemies halted — more from shock than fear.

Coconut stopped them just long enough for Little Tiger to put some distance between himself and the vanguard of the Dog Heads. And then Coconut himself blew the ox horn, which was the signal.

He knew full well what would happen. He was inside when the ropes went up. The elephants milled about in confusion until the Cham mercenaries began to tear down the ropes. As they stopped to do that, the jars began to rain down.

Most of them missed their mark, but some struck the elephants and shattered.

A jar breaking or even a scorpion's sting isn't going to bother an elephant. But out scattered the poisonous insects and lizards and snakes. You can bet that they were angry and hungry from such a long captivity. I think some drivers even got bitten. Others climbed down from their beasts' backs. Still others tried to stay atop the elephants and swat our little scaly warriors away — which made them easy targets for the arrows.

And, of course, the jars that missed the elephants shattered on the ground — right among the Dog Heads.

Dog Heads can be brave, even vicious, but that's when they face a human foe. Warriors from the Five Clans are something else. The vanguard of the Dog Heads stopped being a unit and became a group of desperately hopping individuals. And it's no good stomping on a poisonous bug or snake when you're barefoot.

So they turned and tried to retreat. Of course, the bulk of their war band behind them was still trying to advance. So the two groups collided, resulting in a standstill.

That was when Great-Uncle Sambar struck. His warriors stormed down from either side of the pass. And Little Tiger and his warriors had enough time to put on the boots that had been hidden in a spot further down the pass. They advanced at the same time.

Confused, riderless, the elephants just stood around, which left them as targets for some of our braver warriors. All volunteers. I had watched them practicing before the battle. They crouched down and came at the elephants' bellies. I couldn't picture trying to crawl underneath those giant creatures — let alone prod them with a sword point.

Our warriors didn't kill any of the huge beasts, but the pain made the elephants angry. I don't know how many of those brave men were trampled.

However, the elephants tore up and down the pass.

Our warriors had orders to try to stay out of the elephants' way and let them charge on past. Without a driver, the elephants would simply seek escape and not attack them.

On the other hand, the Dog Heads and Big Rock warriors were not prepared for an elephant charge. They were packed on the floor of the pass. And Great-Uncle Sambar's warriors on either side made sure they stayed there. Most of the elephants headed back for the last, safe place they had known — which was Big Rock. The frightened, angry beasts plowed right through our enemies.

It was a total rout!

The Dog Heads are scuttling back to their mountains. They won't dare show their faces in our land for a long time. They've abandoned the warriors from Big Rock. The traitors surrendered by the hundreds.

I have to stop now. We are heading back to help the wounded.

Peacock doesn't know what happened to Coconut. What a brave fool.

I hope he's all right.

The poets lie. There is no glory in war. Only death and blood.

How many widows and fatherless children will be waiting at home?

And the dead may be better off than the living. Some of the men are maimed for life. Their groans fill the air.

And the smell. I threw up when we came back to the pass. I have tended to wounded at home, but this is the first battlefield I have ever seen.

Begonia and Barbet and the other children are just as sick. I'm sure we're going to have nightmares about what we've seen.

We have to bury the bodies quickly. The only ones who will be happy will be the worms and maggots.

And then there will be a great deal of trash to pick up — enough broken arrows to make a forest. Swords. Spears. And a small hill of broken pottery.

It's one thing to come up with clever plans for a battle. It's another to see what happens when they're carried out.

And this is supposed to be a great victory. I would hate to see what a defeat looks like.

I gazed at an elephant's tracks again. What huge feet. They must have made the ground rumble. Would I have had the courage to face them myself? And I think of the men who actually tried to sneak underneath their bellies. How many of them survived?

Thank heaven, Kumquat's alive. For a change, I got to put the healing salve on her and watch her wince. The Dog Heads managed to fire a volley of arrows into the treetops before the warriors of the Five Clans began their assault.

Even so, she's one of the lucky ones with only an arrow in her arm. Auntie Goral and a dozen of their friends will not be returning home.

Others have broken bones. Some of them are better at climbing up a tree than going down.

The worst was Uncle Muntjac, who fell out of a tree. However, Kumquat says that's his own fault for showing off. He was leaning out too far to get off a shot at a Cham driver and lost his balance.

Uncle Muntjac insists that he got him. Kumquat says he missed. She takes turns scolding and tending his poor broken body.

Little Tiger and Great-Uncle Sambar are all right. They are still wearing their clumsy boots. Since I'm barefoot, I have to watch where I walk. I think Cinnamon Pass will be a deadly area for years. We just dumped all the poisonous bugs, toads, lizards, and snakes from the Great Forest in this area.

But at least we'll be alive to actually walk here.

My brother and great-uncle congratulated me on my plan. Why don't I feel clever? I feel the opposite: If I had really been smart, I would have come up with some scheme to have peace without any killing.

And, anyway, Little Tiger and Great-Uncle Sambar and all the others were the ones who made it work.

No one's seen Coconut.

The area where we sprang the trap is heaped with bodies.

I'm going to look for him there.

Later

He's dead.

He was at the bottom of a pile of corpses.

The boys from the Ape House died in a ring around him. They stayed together even in death.

He still had the ox horn in his hand.

I took the flower from my hair and put it in his.

He would have been a good friend. Perhaps more — if he had lived.

How many more boys will have to die?

239

It's begun to rain again so I'm writing underneath a tree. I have to be careful to avoid the survivors of the Five Clans who are everywhere.

Little Tiger has ordered my little war band to return to Kingfisher Hill. Peacock will herd them along.

However, I'm to stay. My brother actually wants my advice! This is the first time he's ever consulted me. I guess I've won a little respect.

Unfortunately, it's not based on art or philosophy.

It's on revenge. He expects me to come up with some ingenious torture for our prisoners from Big Rock.

I'm so sick of blood. I can't think of shedding more. I've already seen too much suffering and death. Somewhere among our prisoners is some boy like Coconut. I'm just too tired to be mad.

Wait. I mustn't forget that they killed my father. And they murdered Master Chen.

Remember how angry I was when we brought Father's body home? And remember how outraged I was when I found Master Chen dying and then his library being burned? I wanted to take our enemies' heads and worse. My anger was as hot as a fire.

But now . . .

But now there are no flames. Not even coals. Only ashes.

Maybe if I go over and look at the traitors, I can stoke up the fire again.

Later

I expected to see monsters. All I saw were miserable lumps of humanity. They squat in the mud exposed to the pouring rain. Their arms bound behind them. Heads bowed, expecting the worst.

Lord Leopard, who was once so proud, sits apart. I should hate him, but he looks so shocked and frightened. And so I cannot.

I tried to remind myself again of all their crimes. And for one moment, the hate flared up once more.

It tastes so sweet.

But it also feels so ugly.

If Father's ghost were here, would it demand revenge? No, he would want an end to the feuding.

It's the age-old trap that Father was trying to escape: the endless circle of killing and being killed. It's like a rooster fight. We strut and dance about. Then it's a peck for a peck. And a spur slash for a spur slash.

And I remembered what Master Chen said when he came to our village: He was fighting to end fighting.

I hadn't understood it then. But now that I have seen a battlefield, I do.

Do I want this to go on and on?

I kept hearing Mater Chen's last words over and over: The living are more important than the dead. Revenge. Rights and wrongs. Pride. They are not as important as peace.

I hear the boom of thunder. Heaven is sounding its own bronze drum.

Suddenly, I feel like that ancient egg. And something is hatching inside. Not our ancestor. But an idea.

I must talk to Little Tiger.

Later

My big brother can be so stubborn sometimes!

He says that it has always been a head for a head. It's just a question of what is the most satisfying way of killing our enemies.

So I asked him if he wanted to be back here next year.

He said after he was done, there would be no next year for Big Rock. There would not be a male left. And the women and children would be sold as slaves. We would torch the village and poison the fields.

I could see many heads nodding at that.

And part of me was saying that Little Tiger was right. But inside me there was another part screaming "No! No!"

I looked around at all those proud warriors, and suddenly, all I saw were little boys — boys who were scared that everyone would think they were weak.

So out loud I asked Little Tiger what would happen when the rest of the Hsien heard about this revenge.

My brother was smug about it, saying that they would be terrified.

I pointed out that some day the frightened villages would band together and try to do away with Kingfisher Hill before we could visit the same fate upon them. He could rule by fear and might only for so long. Blood only gets more blood. But justice will eventually get justice.

Little Tiger got very testy then. Kindness is a waste of time, he said.

Then I mentioned a story from Master Meng. In his own day, people also said that kindness was useless. But they were like people who try to put out a burning house with just a cup of water. When the house burns down, they say that water cannot stop a fire. And everyone says the same thing about kindness when it doesn't work. That's why they act with cruelty because they think that's the only answer.

If I had not come up with part of the plan for our

victory, I think Little Tiger would have kicked me out of the camp.

He got red in the face and said the Chinese books have weakened my mind.

I'm sorry, Master Chen. You would have been patient and coaxed my brother along the correct path of logic. But I'm a long way from being a philosopher like you. I couldn't keep my temper. Instead, I got so mad that I told my brother that he ought to be glad that I read the Chinese books, otherwise his head would have been decorating some Dog Head camp by now.

That made him even angrier. He said that I have spent too much time with the Chinese. I'm only half-Hsien now.

That insult hurt worse than any knife wound.

Great-Uncle Sambar hastily ended the meeting before we could say worse things. But the damage had been done. The wound is already festering inside me.

Maybe what Little Tiger says is true: I have been changed by my stay among the Chinese. I —

Ugh. What's that awful smell?

I can see Kumquat squatting at a fire. I bet she's brewing one of her awful herbal teas for me. It must be some cure to make me come back to my senses.

I won't drink it.

I think I'm the sensible one.

Later

No, it was for poor Uncle Muntjac. He must really love Kumquat. It's the only reason anyone would drink that horrible stuff.

That evening

Uncle Muntjac has died.

His last words were to me. He said that now no one could think he was a coward.

I agreed. He had proved himself a brave warrior and a true friend.

I will miss him.

Poor Kumquat is weeping. How many other happy couples will be broken up by this war?

Fourth month, twenty-eighth day
Early next morning

It has stopped raining.

I saw my little war band off. They were all very quiet. I think they're glad to be gone from this bloody place.

And yet the rain has washed the sky so clean. It's so blue this morning. So bright. So intense. A kingfisher blue.

It made me think of Father. He would have loved this sky — just like he loved the kingfishers.

And hadn't he protected those little birds when everyone else wanted to kill them?

I don't mean to say that the folk from Big Rock are as nice as the kingfishers. That isn't the point. You have to fight for what you believe is right.

That afternoon

I've just spent half the day arguing with Little Tiger. I'm hoarse now.

I don't care if everyone thinks I'm only half-Hsien.

Is it so monstrous to want a fair and lasting peace?

So even though they look at me more and more oddly, I keep reminding them of how hard Father had worked for peace.

However, my brother keeps pointing out what Father's peacemaking got him.

We are in our own endless dance of words.

I have to stop now to help bury Uncle Muntjac. There won't be time to build a coffin and hold a proper funeral. However, he was a simple man and a soldier. He'll understand.

If it had just been me, I would never have changed Little Tiger's mind. Thank heaven for Kumquat and all the old grannies and aunties.

We all took turns putting a spadeful of wet dirt over Uncle Muntjac, including Kumquat and each of the old ladies.

Soon we were a frightful sight. It had been hard to dig the grave because the ground was so muddy. The sides kept sliding in. All of us were covered in mud. Our topknots had become undone and hung down like dirty ropes.

As we worked, Kumquat sang a lament so sad that we all began to weep. I put my arm around my old nursemaid and started to sing with her. Soon, the other aunties joined in.

When we had finished burying Uncle Muntjac, Kumquat wiped away her tears and turned to Little Tiger who had come to pay his respects.

Grabbing my brother, she told him to listen to me!

All the grannies and aunties crowded in around Little Tiger, scolding him as if he were only five years old. They are siding with me, too.

They're tired of burying sons and grandsons. They're tired of living in fear. They're tired of having to go armed into the fields. They want peace.

Little Tiger says it's a hopeless dream. Weakness will only encourage our enemies to attack.

But I told him that peace wasn't going to be won overnight. However, it was a goal worth working for. And how does he want to be remembered in song — as a butcher who gave us more war or the king who gave us peace?

Fourth month, twenty-ninth day

Little Tiger is going to spare the Big Rock village and most of the common warriors. However, Lord Leopard and his henchmen will have to pay for their treachery. I don't know if that will really end the feud, but perhaps it's prevented something far worse.

Scroll Seven

Third Year of the Chung Ta T'ung Era
fifth month, first day to sixth month,
seventh day

Fifth month, first day
En route to Kingfisher Hill

For the sake of Kumquat and the other older folk as well as the refugees, we have been taking our time going home. Even though the days are getting longer as summer approaches, they can only walk so much.

I should be happy, but my brother's words still hurt. Everyone, of course, is nice to me because I helped win the victory.

I should be savoring my triumph, but I keep thinking about what my brother called me.

Am I really only half-Hsien now?

And do the others agree?

Fifth month, third day

I can hear the drum booming out a greeting from Kingfisher Hill.

It won't be long now.

This is the worst part about winning the battle.

Mother will be waiting.

This may be the last entry in my history. Have I survived the war only to be skinned alive during the peace?

That evening
Kingfisher Hill

Amazing! I'm still breathing.

Mother scolded me — but at the same time she was crying and hugging me. So her words didn't have the sting they should have.

There were ambassadors already waiting for us. The Hsien who were neutral, and especially the allies of Big Rock, already have come to pledge their loyalty to Little Tiger now. And delegates from the other tribes in the Great Forest have been streaming through the gates to discuss treaties.

Peacock has quite forgotten his sufferings during his journey after me. He's in his element now. I think he's the only one who enjoys ceremonies and speech-making.

Little Tiger barely had time to wash off the dust before he had to meet with the envoys. I was going to slip out the back, but my brother asked me to listen with Mother.

I couldn't help feeling resentful after what he said. I asked him why he wanted advice from only a half-Hsien.

Little Tiger apologized, answering that he had spoken in the heat of the moment. So, I could hardly say no.

Why is there more talking in peacetime than in war? Some of the speech-makers are so pompous! Like apes howling in the treetops.

I wish I could snort, but the people in the other room can hear me so I can only complain silently in writing.

And there are more ambassadors on the way. More talk! More boring speeches!

I think I liked it better when Little Tiger didn't want my advice.

Fifth month, eighth day

I haven't had time to write before this.

Despite the constant rain, lords and ambassadors keep arriving.

It's been meetings, meetings, meetings!

And afterward, Mother, Great-Uncle Sambar, Little Tiger, and I discuss what to do.

Fifth month, tenth day

The Dog Heads have sent a messenger through the downpour.

They are begging us for peace.

My first impulse was to demand their corpses as the price of peace. However, I remembered what my mother had said about feuds among the Hsien: They had gone on for so many generations that everyone had forgotten the first wrong. Perhaps our ancestors had taken first blood from the Dog Heads.

I tried to bring that up in the meeting with the others.

However, Little Tiger is set for demanding the head of every tenth man of their tribe. Mother and Great-Uncle Sambar would settle for the head of every hundredth man.

I am doing my best to work for a "civilized" peace.

It's the argument from Cinnamon Pass all over again. I can tell what all three of them are thinking: I've been changed by the Chinese. I'm no longer a true Hsien.

It hurts, but I'm not going to give up. I owe it to Father and Master Chen.

Later

I've just spoken to Mother. I've reminded her of what she told me when Father was first trying to unite the tribes. (Oh, that day seems so long ago.)

She had said that we had to learn to unite with our enemies. We could not continue to rule by brute force.

I could see that my reminder stuck in her throat as much as it did in mine. However, she smiled and said that I have grown up during the war. She will support me.

Fifth month, eleventh day

It is still raining.

I think my brother is sorry he asked me for advice.

However, Mother and I have gotten him to settle for a payment in silver — I estimated how much the Dog Heads had stolen from the silver mine. We don't want them hiring elephants again.

The Dog Heads are also to return Father's head and the heads of his warriors so we may give them a proper burial.

The Dog Heads have to send some of their own people to serve as hostages to guarantee the good behavior of the others. That's a smart strategy that the Chinese demand of hostile groups.

Finally, they're to return all the Chinese colonists who had been taken away as slaves. Perhaps Master Chen's grandchildren, Lin and Yü, will be among them.

Fifth month, twelfth day

More rain.

The Dog Heads can't seem to believe their luck and have accepted our terms.

They seem so gleeful that I'm having my first doubts. Is my brother right and Master Meng wrong? If the Dog

Heads think we're weak, we'll have to fight the war all over again.

fifth month, twenty-second day

The surviving colonists have arrived despite the rain. There must be five hundred of them. They're soaked to the skin. What a pitiful lot. We're making them as comfortable as we can.

I saw Lin and Yü! They are barefoot and in dirty rags. Even so, Yü has made an effort to keep her face clean of dirt. And she has woven a crude hat from leaves to shade her head from the occasional sun and keep her complexion pale.

Lin has lost that bounce he had in his step. He shambles along now like an old man.

However, I can at least keep my word to my teacher.

I've saved what I can of his family.

And I'll give them what little I rescued from their grandfather's library.

It's the one thing I dread.

But it's only right.

Lin is no longer the boy who flew kites, and Yü is no longer the girl who mocked me.

The carefree children are gone. The Dog Heads have killed them as surely as with a knife.

I did not ask about the horrible things through which they have lived. I do not need to. I can see it in their eyes. They have changed. I feel like there are ghosts inside them who peer back at me from behind masks.

All the other survivors have the same eyes.

After they washed, I brought them some of the clothes their family had given me. Yü was grateful to put on the robe and shoes I gave back to her — even if they are slightly worn. Though his robe is a girl's and his arms stick out of the sleeves, Lin is just glad to be wearing silk once more. The shoes, though, will never fit him. I'll see what I can do about getting him some straw sandals from somewhere. Maybe one of the colonists in the first group we rescued will have woven some.

Then I brought them over to the house where their mother was staying. She sat upon the mat staring into space as she usually does now. Francolin was fanning her devotedly.

Lin and Yü rushed to her with glad cries. There are only a few happy reunions like that. Most of the refugees wander about, looking for any friends and family. When they cannot find them, they begin to weep.

Madame, though, does not recognize her own children anymore. She just looks blank.

Lin sat back, upset. I tried to tell him that I was sure she would come to her senses once again. That she just needed her family with her.

Before the Dog Heads' attack, Lin would have smiled, at least. Now, though, he just sat on his heels and rocked back and forth nervously.

Yü, however, began fussing with her Mother's hair and clothes. She gave a start when she saw the hairpin and the mirror.

She turned to me and sulkily asked me if I was going to gloat.

That puzzled me and I asked, Over what?

She said because she had fought so hard not to give the hairpin and mirror to me. Now they are all that remain of the family's treasures. If her mother hadn't given them to me, they would never have been preserved.

I told her I was only trying to pay them back for their kindnesses.

Yü demanded to know what kindness she had ever done me.

With someone else, I might have made up a lie. However, I knew Yü wanted the truth. So I told her that she could have tormented me worse than she had. I was grateful she had taken it so easy on me.

Yü cradled the mirror in her lap. She said she was sorry I had misinterpreted her so badly. She had never meant to be kind. She had wanted to make every moment of my life miserable. If she had failed, it was from lack of imagination rather than from goodwill.

So I asked her what I had done to her to make her hate me so.

She stared down at her own reflection in the mirror. She confessed it hadn't been hate. It had been jealousy.

I remembered my conversation with Madame, who thought Yü was jealous of me for replacing her in her grandfather's affections. And I apologized, saying that I had never meant to do that.

However, she said her mother was wrong. She was jealous of my life!

I am free to do so many things.

I said she could have done them, too.

Yü pointed out bitterly that to do them, she would have had to leave the colony and live with the Hsien, too. Freedom was not worth giving up her standard of living. Chinese girls of her class and status were expected to be marriage fodder. She had despised herself as a coward and had taken out that spite on me.

I sat back on my heels, stunned. So she had envied me all this time.

Captivity has changed both Lin and Yü. How could it not? Life on their estate seems like such a distant dream now.

Together we groomed Madame. Yü was a little reluctant at first to give me instructions. However, after I asked her what to do a few times, she realized I didn't mind. After that, we worked in an easy partnership.

Perhaps it seems foolish to be doing such things in a time of war. And yet it's nice to pretend for a moment that things are back to normal.

I offered her all my robes, but she will only accept a few. Yü still has her pride. She has the most spirit of the Chens. Though she tormented me when I lived with her family, I've almost come to admire her strength and her will.

I gave Lin some money, which he clutched to his chest gratefully. He will use it to start over. They have relatives in the city of Canton to the northeast.

Then I offered Lin the real treasures that I had preserved.

However, he doesn't want the books! He says he has no use for them and nowhere to store them, anyway. It made me both happy and sad at the same time — happy that I can keep them but sorry for my teacher. His books should stay with his family rather than going to a "savage." Master Chen, though, had said I was more Chinese than many colonists. Perhaps he wouldn't have been surprised.

So he knew! He realized what he was doing. He was taking out some of the Hsien from me and putting in the Chinese.

It seems cruel for a follower of the kindly Master Meng.

Who wants to be half-Chinese and half-Hsien?

The Chinese still despise me as a "savage." The Hsien think of me as weak like the Chinese.

What am I? A monster?

Where do I belong?

Sixth month, third day

I have not been able to write because I have spent all this time with Toad and Peacock.

A messenger has come from the Chinese.

The soldiers are returning to Kao-liang. The Liang emperor has crushed the rebel. So he's anxious to reopen the silver mine.

General Feng Jung will arrive tomorrow to discuss a treaty with us. And that has made Peacock ecstatic. There are all these new ceremonies to plan. He has quizzed me about everything I remember about Chinese customs.

They are so much more formal than we are. Peacock is one person who would be happier to be Chinese.

And Toad pesters me every day to get him some new, iron Chinese pots.

One of the books I rescued is a cookbook so I have been translating the recipes for Toad. Of course, he has to practice the dishes, but then I have to sample them. I just hope I can fit back into my robes.

When the general leaves, he will escort the rescued colonists back to what's left of their town.

More Chinese will be coming from the coast to join them. Together they'll rebuild the colony.

The Chinese are not going to leave. So it's best to learn how to get along with them.

Even Little Tiger realizes that now. He wants me to put on my Chinese clothes and act as interpreter again. I don't think he questions the wisdom of sending me to school.

Later

A column of real Chinese soldiers is an impressive sight. There is a snap to them and their faces have the serious look of veterans.

Their iron helmets have side pieces to protect the sides and back of their heads. The common soldiers have shields and vest armor made out of scale-shaped pieces of iron to protect the chest. A long apron of leather strips protects their waist and upper legs. Beneath the armor, they all wear pleated coats of green.

They look like turtles marching on their hind legs. I don't dare laugh at them, though. Their spears and swords and crossbows look wickedly sharp. So these turtles have teeth and claws.

And they march smartly in formation as if they are parts of a machine. But this is a machine that kills.

General Feng Jung looks just as efficient. And so does his young son, Feng Pao. Both of them are wearing suits of armor polished bright as mirrors. It almost hurts my eyes.

And they set up camp just as smartly as they marched.

I have to stop now. The Fengs are ready to talk to my brother.

Later

General Feng Jung is a practical man. He realizes the Chinese must live with us just as we must live with them. So they are offering to recognize our authority over a large part of the Great Forest!

Father's dream is coming true!

And perhaps Master Chen's vision will become real, too.

Time for the banquet.

Mother is drumming again! It's a welcome sight and sound.

But when the banquet is done and the Chinese go back to their camp, I think I'll go to the shed and catch up on my reading.

It's been a long time since I've been able to read for pleasure.

That evening

The general's son, Feng Pao, is funny for a Chinese.

I was sitting inside the shed, quietly reading by the light of a Chinese candle. Now that the Chinese are coming back, I can use candles as much as I like.

The rain, which had begun again, was pattering on the thatch roof. Then Feng Pao came tramping along through the mud.

He said he had heard that I could read.

I was annoyed at being interrupted. Besides, he made me feel like a trained monkey.

I told him that I was not an acrobat doing her tricks, so he should leave me alone.

With a laugh, he asked what the title of my book was.

I held up Master Meng.

He said that from my reputation, he thought I would be reading a book of military strategy.

I told him that I hated fighting.

He said he was surprised because I was so good at it.

I answered that I fought for peace. If I had my way, soldiers like him would be out of work.

He smiled. "And then kings and emperors would have to rule by good example rather than force." He quoted from Master Meng!

It was my turn to be surprised. Why was a warrior reading a peace-loving philosopher?

He said it was the times that made him wear armor rather than a scholar's robes. He said if he had his way he would be sitting beside me reading. Then he asked if he could examine the other books.

When I told him to go ahead, he started to inspect the scrolls. However, he was puzzled by the scorch marks so I told him about the rescue.

He actually bowed to me and thanked me.

He must love books as much as I do.

As he looked at them, he smiled as if he were meeting old friends again. He even knows the grammars!

Master Chen would have loved him as a student, and I told him that.

He confessed that he had wanted to go to Master Chen's

school. However, his father had gotten quite upset and forbidden it. All his family were expected to be soldiers.

Strange. We come from two different worlds, and yet I feel we have so much in common.

I said it was a shame we couldn't have lived in more peaceful times.

He nodded. He said that sometimes when he felt discouraged by the killing, he reminded himself that he was working for just that moment. I felt as if I had been hit with a club. Feng Pao must be considered as odd among the Chinese as I am among the Hsien.

I chose my words with care, asking him if his reading habits hadn't made things difficult for him at times. He laughed because when he was young, he was the despair of his father. He always preferred reading to hunting. He added that all his family thought he was a little weak-minded because of his tastes.

He was eager to learn about Master Chen, and I was happy to tell him. I don't think I've ever had a Chinese — not even Master Chen — make me feel as if I knew more than he did. But then Feng Pao isn't any ordinary Chinese.

For the first time in a long while, I don't feel lonely. I've met a fellow "monster."

Sixth month, fourth day

Feng Pao and I have been talking about books all day while it rains outside.

Even when Kumquat began dusting off the books, we didn't let her distract us.

Odd, though. Up until now, Kumquat could have cared less about the books. Why is she suddenly interested in them?

She started to sing her love tunes again. Maybe she was missing Uncle Muntjac and wanted to take her mind off him.

Sixth month, fifth day

Today we had even more company while we tried to talk. Feng Pao's orderly decided to repair his master's gear by the shed rather than in the camp.

When it started to rain, his orderly jammed inside. It was quite cramped with the four of us in there. However, Feng Pao and I didn't let either Kumquat or the orderly stop us from chatting.

Feng Pao is being sent back to Kao-liang with the first group of colonists.

Why do I feel so sad? It must be the rain that has been falling steadily. Won't it ever stop?

I don't see why such a high-ranking officer as he has to head the escort. After all, the Dog Heads aren't a threat anymore.

He looks just as frustrated as I feel.

He only had enough time to tell me the news because he had to go back to oversee the preparations for the trip.

I told him to take any book he wanted.

I felt a little twinge when he took a scroll of wonder tales. I had been saving that for myself. I hadn't read that one yet. I felt a little sad as I wrapped it to protect it from the downpour.

Afternoon

I asked Kumquat to help me with the books. I wanted to put them into baskets that are more tightly woven. That should preserve them in this damp air.

Why is it that suddenly she doesn't want to leave the

palace and go out in the rain? She hasn't been too busy the last couple of days to go out to the shed.

She told me she had been in the shed on Mother's orders.

Kumquat was my chaperone! And I bet the general sent the orderly for the same purpose!

I snorted and said we just loved books.

Kumquat laughed and said I could call it what I liked, but she had seen the start of enough romances to know one when she saw it. And this was a match that neither the Hsien nor the Chinese want. She sang a bit of a love song about a fish that loved a monkey.

Everyone's being so ridiculous!

Later

I tried to tell Mother that Feng Pao and I were just book lovers.

She's closed her mind on the subject. She has forbidden me to see Feng Pao anymore!

And Little Tiger is acting very much the big brother. He says a Chinese soldier is not good enough for me.

I reminded him that he had said I was half-Chinese already.

His face turned a bright red. He said he wished I would forget that. And he was sorry he had ever spoken those words. He had watched me transform over the last two years from a nice little Hsien girl, and the transformation had scared him. But maybe the other caterpillars were just as uneasy when the first of them changed into a butterfly.

I said he wasn't the boy he had been, either.

He said the times themselves were changing. Sometimes he felt as if I were more in step with them than he was. And then he actually hugged me!

I found myself hugging him back. I don't know what I am, but he's right. I'm not the person I was. And neither is he. Nor are the times.

Still, he won't let me see Feng Pao.

Master Meng never wrote about the drawbacks to peace: When people's minds are idle, they leap to the most foolish conclusions.

Sixth month, seventh day

They've set Kumquat to watch me and make sure I don't say good-bye to Feng Pao. But I know how to put her to sleep. All I have to do is translate a grammar book out loud.

Something on verbs should do nicely.

I had her snoring away five paragraphs into a scroll. Kumquat's made of sterner stuff than me. It takes only three paragraphs to put me to sleep.

I put on a raincoat of straw and slipped outside. It was quite muddy, so I had to watch my step.

Little Tiger and the general were at the Chinese camp to see off the Fengs in the rain.

Didn't they glare when they saw me slog by! But they could hardly say anything in front of the others. It would be an insult to an ally.

Then Lin called to me. Like the other refugees, the Chens wore raincoats of straw that we had given them. I could have found the Chens anyway because they were standing under the bright red umbrellas I had sent out to them. Francolin was there, too, fussing over Madame one last time.

I couldn't help embracing each of them in turn. Madame simply stood there, as unfeeling as a vegetable. Yü, though, has done a wonderful job with Madame. She has taken out her mother's robe so it fits Madame better. And Madame's hair looks far better than anything I had tried to do.

Yü has begun to look stylish again. She has even gotten

a Chinese straw hat from somewhere and decorated the crown with flowers and tied ribbons to the brim.

She has also adapted her brother's robe better to his frame and limbs. And with the tiger belt hook, Lin has begun to look more like his old self, even if he doesn't act that way yet.

I made my farewells to them. They still intend to go on to Canton. Lin has promised to write to me once they have settled somewhere. And I have sworn to write back to my old schoolmate. (Heaven knows when we will get each other's letters, though.)

Yü says she will not settle for a letter. I must come in person and stay with them again. I was so astounded that I could not think of any reply. Lin laughed — the first time I have heard that from him. He says that for once Yü has me at a loss for words.

Yü says that she cannot live with herself if she leaves me stuck in this place. She intends to finish the job of making a proper Chinese lady out of me.

I guess she means well. She might not like the restrictions of her life as a Chinese girl, but she still takes pride in being Chinese.

Yü will never really change. I've come to like it, in a way. The whole world has been stood upon its head, and there are very few things that are constant anymore. Yet a mango will still fall down and not up. The sun still rises in the east and sets in the west. The stars will shine. And I can always count on Yü to insult me.

However, she is stronger than her brother. She'll see that they do all right.

Feng Pao was busy with the last preparations, but he came right over when he saw me. I think he was keeping an eye out for me.

He says he's only borrowing the scroll. He's promised to return it in person as soon as he can.

Then I watched him march off with the Chens and the other survivors. It seems like I'm always saying good-bye to someone.

I don't understand why I felt so happy. I know it's foolish because he might never come back. However, just in case, I'll pick out some books that he might like to read afterward.

All the time that Mother and Little Tiger were scolding me, I was going over titles in my head. When they were finished, Francolin and I returned to the palace.

Good old Kumquat. She's still asleep in my room.

Now that Madame is gone, Francolin immediately wanted to turn her attentions to me, saying I should change my wet clothes. However, I don't want to take off my robe. For some reason, I feel like being Chinese today.

I don't want to forget a thing.

No, I can't sit inside. It's stopped raining. I need sunshine. It matches my mood. So I'll move out to the veranda.

A little later

The veranda is no good. There are too many people around. I need to be alone. Maybe down on the riverbank. With Father.

Later

Oh, it's so perfect. The sunlight is shining off the water below like scales, and the river looks like a great dragon dancing for joy around our village.

And I just saw a young kingfisher flash into the air. It looks like a piece of blue chipped from a rainbow.

And there's another.

There are so many of them. They take such joy in their wings.

I'm glad I wore my blue robe. I've fooled them into thinking I'm a big kingfisher myself. They're flitting around my head. I feel like I'm floating off the ground. And I'll drift higher and higher right into the heart of the sky where the color "blue" was born.

I have to dance!

I'm so out of breath now! Dizzy as well.

But I couldn't help twirling around in circles so my sleeves belled up like wings. I felt like I was flying with them.

So many kingfishers are darting and skipping through the air now. I think they must love the sunshine as much as I do.

Next year perhaps both riverbanks will be filled with nests just like they were in the old days. And then the air will be filled with flashing chips of blue.

Father was right to protect them. Because now there will be a next year for them. And for us.

I —

Writing will have to wait.

Barbet found me and told the others. Hibiscus and Begonia have even woken up poor Kumquat and dragged her out here.

It's hard to write because Drongo's climbing all over me, clamoring for a tale.

Even Mother and Little Tiger have drifted down to the river to join us. They want to hear one, too.

It's such a warm, sunny, drowsy afternoon.

So peaceful.

So full of smiles.

So full of kingfishers. They're circling around. It's almost like part of the sky broke and the pieces are swirling around us.

I feel all warm inside. And safe. And happy.

I can almost feel Father is with us, grinning again.

A perfect time for a story. And I know just the one.

Epilogue

Little Tiger soon came to rule a large area and became very rich and powerful. Unfortunately, he began to believe he could get away with anything. So he would make up excuses to attack his neighbors and plunder them.

Princess Redbird did her best to curb her brother's excesses and prevent war. Finally, exasperated with her brother, people asked her to be their ruler instead.

General Feng Jung came to recognize her virtues, and around A.D. 535 arranged a marriage between Feng Pao and Princess Redbird. After her marriage, she convinced her people to follow more of the Chinese ways. Together with her husband, she ruled wisely and fairly. Chinese or Hsien, lord or peasant, she treated everyone the same — even her relatives.

So by her wisdom and, above all, by her example, she brought law and order to the Great Forest.

This was no small feat in a time of constant war and rebellion that destroyed other powerful kingdoms.

Even after her husband's death, she kept the peace, sometimes with words and sometimes with force of arms. Most of the time, though, the Hsien survived because of her wits. The Emperor of the Ch'en dynasty (which succeeded the Liang) showered her with gifts and honors. Among them was the title, Lady of Ch'iao Kuo, by which she is officially known in the *Standard History of the Sui Dynasty*, the *Sui shu*.

This remarkable woman lived to a ripe old age — no small achievement for the times — and passed away around A.D. 601 surrounded by her grieving kin. Her family, the Fengs, remained prominent in the politics of southern China long after that.

Life in China
in A.D. 531

Historical Note

The Southern Chinese

Southern China lies in the tropical latitudes. In the Lady of Ch'iao Kuo's time, the region was covered by a rain forest and filled with a wide variety of animals such as elephants and rhinoceroses. Since then, farms have replaced the forest and the forest ecosystem has disappeared with the trees.

Though southern China was conquered in the third century B.C., the Chinese did not settle there in large numbers. For centuries, northern China treated the south as England once treated Australia. Southern China was a place to send soldiers, prisoners, political exiles, and restless adventurers. These Chinese intermarried with the local tribes such as the Hsien. It was only during the Mongol invasions of the Sung dynasty (A.D. 960–1279) that the Chinese began to settle southern China in large numbers.

Because of its history, the present-day southern Chinese people are quite different than the northerners. Southern

Chinese tend to be shorter and darker than northerners and they speak separate dialects. Northerners and southerners favor different crops, farming methods, and even social organizations.

As late as the nineteenth century, the southern Chinese had also kept their penchant for feuds. Even to this day they have preserved a tradition of independence, as many notable rebels have emerged from southern China. The most famous is Sun Yat-sen (1866–1925), who replaced the Chinese empire with an American-style republic. The majority of Chinese-Americans trace their roots to southern China.

The Hsien

The official Chinese histories are usually concerned with the crimes and achievements of emperors so it is remarkable that the Chinese historian, Wei Cheng, dedicated almost four pages to the Lady of Ch'iao Kuo.

In part, this is due to the fact that she looked so favorably upon the Chinese and their customs. However, the Lady also embodied the ideal Chinese ruler in many ways. At an early age she was known as a peacemaker. Throughout her life, she tried to be just and fair and lead her subjects by her own example.

However, Wei Cheng also states that when she was

young, the Lady's mind was full of military stratagems, and she commanded troops and conquered people. Even in her sixties, she sometimes had to don armor and lead troops into the field.

Wei Cheng says the Lady's people are the Hsien and that they had already led the other peoples in this region for generations. During her lifetime, the Hsien were a sizable group of over a hundred thousand households, not including those that weren't taxed by the Chinese and who thus are not recorded in history.

In the other official Chinese histories, the Hsien only appear under that name during the Lady's lifetime. Such a huge group does not simply pop up and disappear overnight. Wei Cheng (580–643), the author of the *Standard History of the Sui Dynasty,* probably used a name that was common during his time but not in others.

Though there is a Feng clan among a minority tribe known as the Yao. They seem to have migrated later into the area. And the characteristics that Wei Cheng lists for the Hsien better fit a people now known as the Li, or the Loi.

More importantly, another history places the Li in the Kao-liang area at around the Lady's time.

Furthermore, Hainan Dao, an island off the south China coast, was quick to submit to the Lady, despite its previous history of fierce independence. Then, as now, the

Li were present in large numbers on that large island. If she were of the same ethnic group, they would have found her authority more acceptable.

I should also note that the Chinese character for the Lady's people, the Hsien, is pronounced as "hsi" in modern Mandarin but "hsien" in medieval times.

History

China had first risen to its greatest glory under the Han dynasty (206 B.C.–220 A.D.). The Han solidified China into an empire and over the centuries oversaw brilliant accomplishments in the arts, science and architecture.

The ethical philosophy of Confucius (551–479 B.C.) permeated the government policy of the Han. A follower of Confucius, Master Meng (371–289 B.C.), or Mencius in the West, also had some influence.

However, like its contemporary, the Roman empire, the Chinese empire fell apart from internal rebellions and barbarian invasions. In 531 A.D., China was still in its dark ages, divided in the north, south, east and west between various groups claiming the imperial throne.

In southern China alone, the Lady lived through three different changes of dynasty: the Liang, the Ch'en, and the Sui.

The various wars and rebellions devastated the Chinese

population in southern China. The Lei-chou peninsula, which lay to the west of the Lady's area, was a rich source of pearls so the Chinese always attempted to hold onto it. However, the taxable population (both Chinese and non-Chinese) dropped from 23,000 households (25–220 A.D.) to just 938 households (420–477 A.D.).

As a result of war, geographical boundaries and names also shifted continually, reflecting the political realities of what the Chinese did and did not control.

And yet in the midst of the widespread destruction, new ideas and inventions were making their own impact. Among other things, paper finally became widespread by the fifth century A.D. — though it had first been invented in 105 A.D.

The Chinese Calendar

The Chinese calendar is based on the moon, while the western calendar is based on the sun. This means that the days and months in each system differ.

Moreover, in China, years are numbered according to a reign title. When a new emperor sat upon the throne, he chose a new name for the era of his rule. The new Liang emperor was in his third year of rule at the time of this diary.

So the first entry of the diary is the first day of the

second month of the third year of the Chung Ta T'ung Era. This corresponds to March 4, 531 A.D. The diary ends on the seventh day of the sixth month, or July 6, 531 A.D.

The Lady's birth date is an approximation. History says she married Feng Pao in the beginning of the Great Unity of the Liang Dynasty, which ranges from 535 to 546 A.D. I have assumed that she was 20, which would most likely place her birth in 516 A.D.

Measurements

As set by the Han dynasty, a ch'ih was equal to 23 centimeters or 9¼ inches. However over the centuries, different dynasties have changed the standard. Today the modern ch'ih is equal to 14.1 English inches or .3581 meters.

A li was equal to 360 paces or 1890 feet.

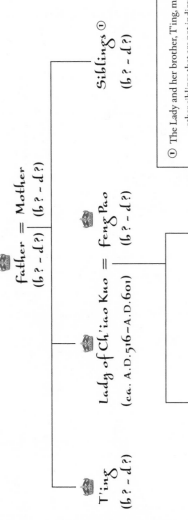

father = Mother
(b? – d?) (b? – d?)

T'ing
(b? – d?)

Lady of Ch'iao Kuo = Feng Pao
(ca. A.D. 516–A.D. 601) (b? – d?)

Siblings ①
(b? – d?)

Feng P'u
(A.D. 552–ca. A.D. 583)

Siblings ②
(b? – d?)

Feng Hun ③
(b? – d?)

Feng Hsüan ③
(b? – d?)

Feng Ang ③
(b? – d?)

① The Lady and her brother, T'ing, may have had other siblings that are not indicated here.

② The Lady and her husband, Feng Pao, may have had more than one child besides Feng P'u, but their names and dates are not known.

③ Exactly who the parents of the Lady's three grandchildren are is undetermined. Their relationship to one another is also undetermined.

The Lady of Ch'iao Kuo's Family Tree

The Chinese, like the Romans and recent colonial empires such as the English, made alliances with powerful tribes on their borders to create buffers. In exchange for recognizing the authority of the Chinese and some form of tribute, a frontier tribe was allowed to govern itself though the ruler might have an official title from the Chinese. In times of political chaos, these tribes would be self-governing for all intents and purposes. Throughout much of her life, the Lady was the ruler of a large region, in fact, if not in official Chinese title.

The Hsien were one of the foremost tribes in southern China in the sixth century, but their rulers remain faceless and nameless for the most part. However, in the Chinese histories, the Lady's brother is given the Chinese name of T'ing.

The Lady married Feng Pao, the son of Feng Jung whose grandfather, Feng Yeh, had settled in the region with some of his troops. She had at least one son, Feng P'u, and three grandsons, Feng Hun, Feng Hsüan, and Feng Ang. However, it is not known if any of them are directly descended from Feng P'u or what the relationships are among them. Dates of birth and death (when available) are noted. The chart illustrates what is known of her actual family. The crown symbol indicates those who ruled over the region. Double lines represent marriages or partnerships; single lines indicate parentage.

T'ing

Lady of Ch'iao Kuo's older brother. His oppressive acts led his subjects to replace him with the Lady.

Lady of Ch'iao Kuo

The ruler of a large part of southern China for most of her long life.

Feng Pao

Grand Protector of Kao-liang at the time that he married the Lady. At his death, revolt broke out all over southern China, which the Lady ended. Many years later, he was posthumously granted the title Duke of Ch'iao Kuo after his wife and grandson helped end a revolt.

Feng P'u

Son of the Lady and Feng Pao. With his mother, he helped crush a revolt by a Chinese rebel. Many honors were bestowed upon him and his mother.

Feng Hun

Grandson of the Lady. He served on diplomatic missions.

Feng Hsüan

Grandson of the Lady. The Lady sent him with an army to rescue a Chinese garrison besieged by rebels. However, he sided with the rebels and refused to attack, so the Lady put him into prison and replaced him with Feng Ang. At the end of the revolt, though, he was pardoned because of his grandmother's loyal acts and given a new position.

Feng Ang

Grandson of the Lady. After he replaced Feng Hsüan, he successfully completed the mission and went on to help crush the rest of the revolt. He was made the Regional Chief of Kaochou and his grandmother received the title Lady of Ch'iao Kuo, as well as other honors, gifts, and authority.

Princess Red Bird, the Lady of Ch'iao Kuo, lived so many thousands of centuries ago in the dark ages of China that no images exist of her today. Born about A.D. 516, she died around A.D. 601. Her life spanned various dynasties that arose in the sixth to the early seventh centuries: the Wei, the Liang, the Ch'en, and the Sui. Today, we depend on rare artifacts from such ancient dynasties to inform us of the people and culture of long ago China. This sixth century Chinese terra-cotta pottery, "The Noble Woman," from the Musée Cernuschi in Paris, France, gives some impression of how the Lady may have appeared in later years.

290

A map of modern China. Part of the Great Forest, home to the Lady of Ch'iao Kuo, was located in the province of Kwangtung/Guangdong.

A modern photograph of the Great Wall of China. Hostilities between rival clans continued throughout Princess Red Bird's lifetime, until China was reunited in the sixth century under the Sui Dynasty. The Great Wall of China, erected of earth and stone, is said to have been started around 221 B.C. by the first emperor of the Ch'in Dynasty, Shih Huang Ti, as a defense against rebel troops. Throughout later centuries and dynasties, the Wall was extended along China's northern and northwestern border and portions remain intact today.

This earthenware sculpture from the Royal Ontario Museum in Toronto, Ontario, Canada, depicts three warriors from the Wei Dynasty, circa A.D. 525.

This relief print illustrates a panoramic view of the layout of a wealthy Chinese family's estate, not unlike the estate of Master Chen. The main house on the left could be reached by going through two courtyards. Also on the left were the domestic rooms, including the kitchen, which were separate from the principal quarters. This drawing is based on a brick engraving representing a large dwelling in the Sichuan province during the Han Dynasty.

A relief print of the interior view of a schoolroom from the Han Dynasty. The teacher is seated on a platform under a canopy, surrounded by his students, who are seated on mats on the floor.

Glossary of Characters

(* indicates fictional characters)

THE LADY'S FAMILY

    Father

    Mother

    Little Tiger, the Lady's older brother

    *Hibiscus, the Lady's little sister

    *Drongo, the Lady's little brother

    *Begonia, the Lady's little sister

    *Barbet, the Lady's little brother

THE HSIEN

    *Peacock, the royal steward

    *Auntie Goral, a potter

    *Coconut, Little Tiger's best friend

    *Kumquat, the Lady's nursemaid

    *Uncle Muntjac, the Lady's guard

    *Toad, the royal chef

    *Francolin, the Lady's maid

    *Great-Uncle Sambar, adviser to Little Tiger

    *Lord Leopard, ruler of Big Rock

THE CHINESE

> * Master Chen, the Lady's teacher
>
> * Madame, Master Chen's daughter-in-law
>
> * Lin, Madame's son
>
> * Ch'ai, Madame's elder daughter
>
> * Yü, Madame's younger daughter
>
> * Chou, Master Chen's gatekeeper
>
> * Chi, Master Chen's chef
>
> * Wu, Master Chen's steward
>
> * Mei, Madame's maid
>
> * Ming, a trader
>
> * The Sungs, friends of the Chens
>
> * Magistrate, ruler of the town
>
> General Feng Jung, a Chinese officer
>
> Feng Pao, his son

ADDITIONAL CHARACTERS

> * Mustafa, an Arab trader

About the Author

When Laurence Yep first began researching his Chinese identity over thirty years ago, he thought it would be a simple matter of tracing a straight line back into the past. Instead, he found his roots were a dense tangle; for the southern Chinese were created by the fusion of many different groups, including the people who are called Chinese in the diary but who would have called themselves the Han.

Then, too, civil war — such as during the period of the Lady — isolated southern China from the rest of China. As a result, the region turned to other countries for trade, ideas, and folklore. The result is a culture, language, and mythology as distinctive as its cuisine.

He was especially intrigued by the folktales of southern China and has written about it in two other Scholastic books. He wrote about the pearl fisheries of Lei-chou peninsula in *The City of Dragons;* and in *The Boy Who Swallowed Snakes,* he retold a humorous story about the old magic that Kumquat practices in the diary.

He also discovered how many strong women were featured in both the folklore and history of southern China — women such as his mother and those he had known in Chinatown, including his grandmother and aunts.

The Lady of Ch'iao Kuo especially intrigued him because not only was she such a dynamic, resilient figure but because she shared characteristics with modern Chinese-Americans. She blended two different cultures together in her soul but did so in a way that created a new future, flourishing in a time of violent change, when one world was giving way to another.

The Lady's story was especially difficult to tell because the primary source — the *Sui shu,* or *Standard History of the Sui Dynasty* — was in medieval Chinese and the secondary sources were chiefly in German and French.

Moreover, the medieval Chinese culture was quite different than the modern one he knew. Among other things, chairs were still being introduced and tea had not yet become a popular beverage. The ecology of the region also bore little resemblance to present times. All this made the research for this book one of the most complex, and yet despite the difficulties it was also one of the most satisfying to write.

Laurence Yep has published over fifty books, including a Star Trek novel and many prize-winning children's books, including the Newbery Honor-winning *Dragon-*

wings and *Dragon's Gate.* He has also written plays, which have been performed off Broadway, at the Kennedy Center, and at Lincoln Center. In addition to winning an NEA fellowship, he taught at the University of California, Berkeley and the University of California, Santa Barbara.

He lives in central California with his wife, Joanne Ryder, who is also a writer.

Acknowledgments

My thanks to the patient, hardworking Ng Kum Hoon who translated the medieval Chinese and tried to untangle the geography for me. If there are mistakes, it is in my interpretation rather than in his translation. I also wish to thank my patient wife, Joanne, who only saw the back of my head while I was writing.

Cover painting by Tim O'Brien

page 290: Noble Woman, Chinese, sixth century (terra–cotta). Housed in the Musée Cernuschi, Paris, France. Bridgeman Art Library, New York, New York.

page 291: Map of modern China, James McMahon.

page 292: (top) The Great Wall of China. Granger Collection, New York, New York

page 292: (bottom) Chinese Funerary Sculpture of Guardian Warriors. Photographed by Richard Swiecki. Housed in the Royal Ontario Museum. Corbis Images, New York, New York.

page 293: Relief drawing of panoramic view of estate based on an engraved brick representing a large dwelling in the Sichuan province during the Han Dynasty. From Everyday Life in Imperial China by Michael Loewe. (London: Reprinted by B.T. Batsford, a division of Chrysalis Books, 1968). Drawing by Eva Wilson, figure 51, page 139.

page 294: Relief drawing of a teacher and his pupils. From Everyday Life in Imperial China by Michael Loewe. (London: Reprinted by B.T. Batsford, a division of Chrysalis Books, 1968). Drawing by Eva Wilson, figure 10, page 44.

Other books in The Royal Diaries series

ELIZABETH I
Red Rose of the House of Tudor
by Kathryn Lasky

CLEOPATRA VII
Daughter of the Nile
by Kristiana Gregory

MARIE ANTOINETTE
Princess of Versailles
by Kathryn Lasky

ISABEL
Jewel of Castilla
by Carolyn Meyer

ANASTASIA
The Last Grand Duchess
by Carolyn Meyer

NZINGHA
Warrior Queen of Matamba
by Patricia C. McKissack

KAIULANI
The People's Princess
by Ellen Emerson White

VICTORIA
May Blossom of Britannia
by Anna Kirwan

To Lee,
who will also find some battles.

While The Royal Diaries are based on real royal figures
and actual historical events, some situations and people
in the book are fictional, created by the author.

Copyright © 2001 by Laurence Yep

All rights reserved. Published by Scholastic Inc.
555 Broadway, New York, NY 10012.
SCHOLASTIC, THE ROYAL DIARIES, and associated logos are trademarks
and/or registered trademarks of Scholastic Inc.

No part of this publication may be reproduced, or stored in a retrieval system,
or transmitted in any form or by any means, electronic, mechanical, photo-
copying, recording, or otherwise, without written permission of the publisher.
For information regarding permission, write to Scholastic Inc., Attention:
Permissions Department, 555 Broadway, New York, NY 10012.

Library of Congress Cataloging-in-Publication Data
Yep, Laurence.
Lady of Ch'iao Kuo : Warrior of the South / by Laurence Yep.
p. cm. — (The royal diaries)
Includes bibliographical references.
Summary: In 531 A.D., a fifteen-year-old princess of the Hsien tribe in southern
China keeps a diary which describes her role as liaison between her own people
and the local Chinese colonists, in times of both peace and war.
ISBN 0-439-16483-4
1. China — History — Liang dynasty, 502–557 — Juvenile fiction.   [1. China —
History — Liang dynasty, 502–557 — Fiction.   2. Princesses — Fiction.
3. Minorities — Fiction.   4. Identity — Fiction.   5. War — Fiction.
6. Diaries — Fiction.]   I. Title.   II. Series.
PZ7.Y44 Lad 2001
[Fic] — dc21   00-051617

10 9 8 7 6 5 4 3 2 1   01 02 03 04 05

The display type was set in Braganza
The text type was set in Augereau
Book design by Elizabeth B. Parisi
Photo research by Zoe Moffitt

Printed in the U.S.A.   23
First printing, September 2001